Zoe's
Extraordinary
Holiday Adventures

ZOE'S EXTRAORDINARY HOLIDAY ADVENTURES

Christina Minaki

Second Story Press

Library and Archives Canada Cataloguing in Publication

Minaki, Christina, 1977-
Zoe's extraordinary holiday adventures / by Christina Minaki.

ISBN 978-1-897187-26-5

I. Title.

PS8626.I526Z62 2007   jC813'.6   C2007-903657-0

Edited by Gena Gorrell
Cover photographs © Laura Bombier
Design by Melissa Kaita

Special thanks to Caroline Rossignol and Georgia

Printed and bound in Canada

*Second Story Press gratefully acknowledges the support of the Ontario Arts
Council and the Canada Council for the Arts for our publishing program. We
acknowledge the financial support of the Government of Canada through the
Book Publishing Industry Development Program.*

 Canada Council   Conseil des Arts
for the Arts   du Canada

ONTARIO ARTS COUNCIL
CONSEIL DES ARTS DE L'ONTARIO

Published by
Second Story Press
20 Maud Street, Suite 401
Toronto, Ontario, Canada
M5V 2M5
www.secondstorypress.ca

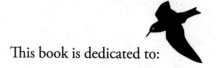

This book is dedicated to:

My parents, Frances and Mike Minaki, and my sister, Nicole Minaki-Farrar, for building my foundation with the essentials: love, faith, strength, hope, and books.

Tina Bauer, for being so full of life and love, so ready for anything...including me! You are my six degrees of freedom.

Michelle Benincasa, a passionate woman of brilliance, boldness, and dignity, for supporting me through Zoe's growth process, and so many other milestones over the years.

And to...the children I love, who are already amazing: William Michael Farrar, Peter and Heather Watt, Stavroula and Alkisti Krisila, and Jordan Komakech.

CONTENTS

Chapter One

HALLOWEEN QUEEN

Zoe was ready for anything. But what she wanted most of all was an adventure.

Ella, on the other hand, was having second thoughts.

"Come on," Zoe coaxed gently. "I'm the queen and you're my court jester. You *have* to wear the hat! It's Halloween! We've gotta go, Ella...you don't want to miss all the fun, do you?"

"I'm sure she doesn't, but maybe she'd rather go out as a wolf," Aunt Beth suggested as she came into Zoe's bedroom.

"I don't think so. She's way too cuddly for a wolf. I'm a queen and I need my court jester. Besides, everyone at school today loved our costumes. Can you help me keep this hat on Ella's head, please? I can't get these clasps done up right."

"I'll bet you guys were a hit at school," Aunt Beth said as she came closer and took over with the dog. "You're a lovely queen, and your wheelchair makes a beautiful throne."

As Aunt Beth fiddled with the hat, Zoe thought about how strange it was to call her wheelchair beautiful. It helped Zoe get around, so it was useful. But *beautiful?*

Now, Ella was beautiful — a gorgeous, chocolate brown Labrador retriever with soulful brown eyes that made Zoe melt. Ella knew all Zoe's secrets, even the ones so special that not one person knew them — not her mother or father, not her brother, Simon, not her teacher in grade four, Mrs. Green, not even her best friend, Anna.

Ella was such a good girl that Zoe had to reward her somehow. She was an amazing dog, trained at a special dog-school to help Zoe with some of the everyday things she couldn't do on her own. There had even been a graduation ceremony afterward, when Ella had been given a diploma!

Having Ella as her very own made it easier somehow for Zoe that she had trouble walking or using her hands properly. Having Ella there always calmed Zoe down when she was frustrated. The dog never lost her patience because Zoe moved more slowly and stiffly than other kids did. Ella never got annoyed when it was hard for Zoe to tie knots, or cut with scissors, or do up buttons. Ella saw that Zoe didn't find these things easy, but she knew that those problems didn't change how smart Zoe was, or how much Zoe loved her. Ella trusted Zoe.

"I think we're done here," Aunt Beth said, stepping back to admire the bright red, blue, green, and yellow court jester's hat now sitting securely on Ella's head. With the floppy hat, the matching ruffled collar and the bells that Zoe's mother had attached to Ella's harness, the dog was finally ready for her queen. "I don't know if she'll ever forgive you for this, Zoe," said Aunt Beth. "All the dogs will laugh for weeks!"

Zoe thought about that for a moment. It was true that Aunt Beth knew all about dogs. She had a beautiful black poodle named Maggie, and before Maggie there had been Sydney, a large, kind German shepherd. And Aunt Beth was always looking out for Ella. But no one knew Ella better than Zoe, and Zoe was sure Ella was too proud to care what other dogs thought of her costume.

"A court jester is supposed to be funny," Zoe pointed out. "And Ella will survive being laughed at. She has dignity."

Aunt Beth smiled. "So has her queen," she said.

✦✦✦

They made quite a trick-or-treating crew: Zoe the queen, Ella the court jester, Anna the ladybug and Simon the magician. Zoe's mom and aunt were good and evil witches.

"What did you get from Mrs. Scott?" Zoe asked Anna.

"The usual…gummy bears."

"She gave me my favorite," Zoe said, beaming. "Red licorice. Want some?" she asked, reaching into the royal pillowcase tied to her wheelchair. It held all her candy.

"Sure."

"I *love* your costume."

Zoe looked up, and smiled at the compliment from yet another neighbor. "Don't let this go to your head, but you look wonderful! Oh, my goodness! What have you done to Ella? And Anna, look at you…how creative!"

"I'm a ladybug."

Zoe wore a long, shimmering purple dress, a jade-green necklace, bracelet, and earrings, and a sparkling tiara. To turn her wheelchair into a throne, her mom and Anna's mom had covered it with silver and royal blue material. Yes, she had to admit that even her boring wheelchair looked fantastic.

The next house was the Jensens'. The best on the block, and everyone knew it. The Jensens made their house seem positively haunted on Halloween. There were bats, carved pumpkins with freaky faces, skeletons, scary music, and a scarecrow in the yard. But there was one difference this year. The Jensens had moved from the townhouse complex where Zoe had been able to roll up to the doorway.

Now they had five steps up to their front door.

Now Zoe couldn't ring the doorbell of the best Halloween house on the block.

She was used to Simon or Anna going up to houses she couldn't get to, to bring her candy. Or to people coming down to their driveway to see her costume and give her treats. But the Jensens, the best house on the block….

Some queen, Zoe thought.

"Trick or treat!"

"Trick or treat!"

"Give me something good to eat!"

"I'm gonna ring the doorbell."

"No, let me!"

"No, I want to ring it!"

Not as much as I do, thought Zoe.

✗✗✗

It wasn't hard to see that Zoe was suddenly unhappy.

"You know, honey, you're doing really well at learning to climb stairs in physio," her mom pointed out. "Maybe you can — "

"No *way!*"

"Don't talk to me like that! If you won't even try, we'll just have to ask the Jensens to come to you."

Zoe felt trapped. The worst of it was that she knew she could climb those stairs, with help. She was learning how in her physiotherapy training at the hospital clinic, and she was doing well, her mom said. The climbing was hard work, and each week Zoe was tired and sweating afterward. But Melissa, her physiotherapist, was always kind and funny. She made Zoe laugh, and she insisted that making a mistake was no big deal, as long as Zoe kept trying.

But Zoe knew she looked weird when she tried to climb stairs. She had to concentrate so hard on making her legs do what they were supposed to. Her feet wanted to drag. It was a lot of work to lift them up to each step. Sometimes they even got stuck under a stair. Climbing the Jensens' stairs with all the trick-or-treaters gawking at her would feel like being on public display.

Zoe thought of the way people examined clothes in a store, on a rack or a mannequin. They made comments like "What a shame! That skirt would be just perfect, if only the pocket didn't look all wrong."

What if the neighbors watched her and thought, *What a shame! Zoe would be just perfect, if only....*

She didn't want anyone feeling sorry for her. But how could she explain that to her mother?

Here goes nothing, she thought.

"Mom, anyone could see me out here. Any kid from school, kids I don't even know. I'd stick out like a clown's nose! They'd stare at me and I'd get scared and hot and prickly, and then I wouldn't do it right. With everyone staring, I'd feel like I was in a zoo!"

Her mom sighed, but when she spoke she was sympathetic. "Zoe, I'm sorry. I can imagine how that makes you feel. But don't you think you stand out when you wait down here for someone to bring you candy?"

You're not helping, Zoe thought. Out loud she said, "Yeah, but at least it's over faster that way."

"Well, then we're back to where we started. We'll ask the Jensens to come down to you."

"No!"

"Aw, Zoe, hurry up already," Simon begged. "Let's *go*."

Zoe's mom and aunt exchanged a look.

"Simon, Zoe has to work this one out on her own, without pressure from you or anyone else," Aunt Beth interjected. "And don't whine, please. For goodness' sakes, you're twelve years old now!"

Then she turned to Zoe. "This one is up to you. You have to choose one or the other. But maybe it would help to think of it this way. If people stare when you climb those steps, at least you'll be doing something new, something to bring yourself closer to the fun. Wouldn't that feel better?"

"Thanks a lot, Aunt Beth," Zoe said. But she was thinking, *It's not that easy.*

Silence fell as Zoe struggled to decide. As she scratched Ella behind the ear, she felt truly alone. Not even her dog, who did so much for her, could make this easier.

Ella picked things up for Zoe when she dropped them on the floor. She walked just in front of Zoe in crowds, to clear a space for her and her wheelchair. She opened doors and drawers, and turned lights on and off with her paws. She went for help when Zoe was stuck and needed a person to do something for her.

She followed Zoe's commands, but she also often seemed to know what Zoe wanted without being told, like when Zoe dropped her book and Ella gave it back to her before anyone else even knew it was on the floor.

But as hard as Ella worked, there were still times, like this very moment, when there was little the dog could do. Ella couldn't hold Zoe up while she climbed stairs. And she certainly couldn't make Zoe's mind up for her about whether to climb them at all.

As she looked down at Ella, a little voice in Zoe's head whispered, *You do want an adventure, don't you?*

≺≺≺

"I know you can do it." Anna assured her, as Zoe pushed her wheelchair to the foot of the Jensens' stairs and locked her brakes.

"Thanks," Zoe said, halfheartedly.

"Are you ready for this, kiddo?" asked Aunt Beth, as Mom put her arm around Zoe.

"I'm not sure."

But somehow she found herself standing with her hand gripping the stair railing, her mom beside her, an arm around her waist. Zoe's hand shook. Her legs shook.

Zoe closed her eyes for a moment and thought of what Melissa said when they worked on the stairs in physio. *Take deep breaths. You're going to straighten one leg, bend the other and lift it to the next step. Breathe. Straighten. Bend. Lift.* The sounds of laughter and trick-or-treating faded around her. *Breathe. Straighten. Bend. Lift.* One step at a time.

She opened her eyes and suddenly she was doing it for real, right in front of the Jensens' house. Mom and Aunt Beth were encouraging her as she went, and she could feel Anna and Simon holding their breath behind her. But she couldn't think about them, or about the cold sweat dripping down her arms. She tried not to think about falling. She tried not to imagine knocking her mom or her aunt down the stairs as she tumbled to the ground. She would *not* crash! She forced herself to think of reaching the Jensens' porch, and tried not to wobble. She coaxed her feet clear of the lip of each stair. Her toes would *not* get stuck.

One step…two…three….

Breathe. Straighten. Bend. Lift. Two more to go.

"Hey, look at the crazy way that girl walks!"

"Where?"

"Over there, on the stairs. What's wrong with her?"

Zoe froze, and felt tears pricking her eyes.

Some stupid queen I am, she thought. *Some adventure!*

Zoe made it to the Jensens' door, but she felt no joy. Halloween was ruined.

Chapter Two
NO SURPRISES

Zoe held the skipping rope carefully, and tried to sound enthusiastic as she chanted the rhyme with her friends.

"Mother may I...."

I wish my legs could skip, she thought. *I just won't watch her feet*, she promised herself, staring hard at the whirling rope instead. But after a few moments, she couldn't help it. Her eyes followed Ruby's feet as they touched the ground and pushed off, again and again, as Ruby jumped, her long black braids flying, her cheeks rosy.

And somewhere deep inside, Zoe hurt.

But then Ella licked her hand, and Zoe heard Anna's voice ring out:

"I want to play tag now, and Zoe's *it!*"

With Anna pushing her wheelchair as fast as she could, off they went. Ella bounded happily beside them.

✘✘✘

It wasn't that her parents didn't hug her as usual, or pay attention when she read them the funny poem she had made up about Ella.

It wasn't that Mom didn't draw a silly happy-face, as she always did, with the jelly on Zoe's bread and peanut butter.

It wasn't that Dad didn't tickle her while she read the third chapter of *Charlotte's Web*, or that Simon didn't race around the house with her in her wheelchair. It wasn't that Ella didn't chase after them with her tail wagging, barking and woofing until Mom stopped laughing and called, "Quiet!"

It wasn't that her parents were any less patient than every other day while they helped Zoe with her exercises.

No, it wasn't that anything was really *wrong*. It was just...*ordinary*. It had all happened before. Every day was exactly the same.

Where is my adventure? Zoe wondered.

✦✦✦

"William and I saw Rufus today," Simon announced at dinner that night. William was Simon's best friend.

Mom put down her fork deliberately and looked at Simon hard. "You didn't go near him, did you?"

"No, we were careful. He's close by, though. I think he lives in Nalini's yard."

"Any skunk that gets in Nalini's way is in for trouble," Dad pointed out, with a chuckle. Nalini was Ruby's grandmother. She was sweet and eager, a little woman with a big heart. Nalini was excited about life. She was always going somewhere, doing something, looking to laugh and have fun…and ready to tell you exactly what she thought of anything, whenever you asked, and sometimes when you didn't! Anytime there was a problem, Nalini could think of ways to fix it, and then roll up her sleeves and get it fixed. If she thought someone was not being treated kindly, or someone hadn't done the right thing, well then, she would speak up and that was all there was to it. And if there was trouble in the neighborhood, Nalini would just take care of it.

If Rufus was living in Nalini's yard, he was one skunk who didn't know what was good for him, and that was that.

"Do you remember the time Nalini found the mouse sleeping on top of her television?" Simon asked.

"Who could forget?" Zoe said. "Everyone for blocks around probably heard her scream!" That same afternoon, Nalini had brought a kitten home from the animal shelter — a little boomerang of orange fur that only stayed still when he was asleep, getting rested for the next burst of activity. Nalini named him Mustang — "He gallops like a little wild horse," she explained — and he soon matured into a perfect cat for her. Nalini was a "no-nonsense" person, and Mustang became a "no-nonsense" cat.

Mustang took care of Nalini's mouse problem in such a short time that she was soon lending him out to anyone in the neighborhood who needed him.

"I guess the mice that Mustang chased out of Nalini's house didn't warn Rufus about him."

"Mom, think about it. Which self-respecting skunk would take advice from a mouse?" asked Simon.

When everyone around the table had stopped laughing, their father said seriously, "Simon, be careful, please. Stay away from that skunk. Getting sprayed by a skunk is no joke!"

"Don't worry, Dad," Simon said. "If Rufus tries to spray me, I'll run. You know how fast I run."

Yeah, he can run, thought Zoe. *They can all run.*

She barely heard the rest of the conversation. All of a sudden she didn't want to eat anymore.

✖✖✖

Anna was coming over after dinner.

From sunset every Friday until sunset every Saturday, Anna had to be with her family to celebrate the Jewish Sabbath. She wasn't allowed to visit then, so she visited Zoe on Thursdays instead. She always slept over, and traveled to school with Zoe on Friday morning. Then they spent the day together in class, and afterwards Anna hurried to get home before the sun went down. Anna's mom said that Anna and Zoe were like two very special dresses: different in some ways, but both beautiful. Anna was one of Zoe's most favorite people.

✖✖✖

"Do you remember when Ella stole Peter's cheddar cheese right off the table?" asked Anna.

Zoe rolled her eyes. Ella was not allowed to share other people's food. There were lots of rules the dog was supposed to obey, because her job was taking care of Zoe and she had to pay attention. She wasn't allowed to chase squirrels. She couldn't chase balls except in her own yard.

On the other hand, Ella could go everywhere with Zoe, even to places where regular dogs were never allowed, like the library and the grocery store. But one day, sitting quietly in the school cafeteria and watching Peter eat cheese and crackers at lunch, Ella had had a bad-dog moment. She had put her paws on the table, flicked out her long pink tongue and gobbled up the whole piece of cheese! Everyone had laughed, even Peter. Even Zoe, although she knew she needed to scold Ella.

Zoe smiled, remembering. "Mrs. Green said it just showed that Ella's still a dog, after all."

Zoe and Ella got along so well, and Ella did such a great job, that sometimes it was easy to forget there wasn't a person hiding under that chocolate fur.

★★★

"I spy with my little eye something that is...green."

The girls had gone to bed, but there was still enough light for them to see. Zoe was lying beside Anna, trying to pay attention to the game, but it wasn't working.

"Ziggy," she said flatly. She wasn't really thinking of Ziggy the frog, her favorite stuffed animal. She was busy thinking of Simon playing hockey, and Anna skating and taking ballet classes.

It wasn't that she didn't want her brother to enjoy hockey and her best friend to love ballet. She was happy for them both. It was just that it seemed so easy to have adventures — really fun, happy, exciting adventures — when you could dance and skate. No one ever knew what would happen next at hockey practice, or skateboarding, or on a ski slope, or even biking in the forest.

Zoe *always* knew what would happen next. Whenever she wanted to try something new, her parents worried that she would fall, or get lost, or get too cold or too hot or too tired. They even made sure she wore the seatbelt attached to her wheelchair, all the time.

There just weren't any real *surprises*.

Chapter Three
THE CHRISTMAS TREE

*W*hen *my hair gets long enough, I'm going to wear it in a braid just like Mrs. Green's,* Zoe said to herself. She was sure she had the best teacher in the world. Mrs. Green was smart and friendly, and she always had great ideas.

"Boys and girls, I have some exciting news!" Mrs. Green was saying now. "Many of you have come here from different countries and cultures, and you know that different people celebrate what is important to them in different ways. For the next few weeks, we are going to talk about how people of many cultures celebrate their annual traditions, often around the same time of year. We are going to learn about how Christians celebrate Christmas, which is sometimes called a Festival of Lights...."

Good, Zoe thought, *any holiday but Halloween.* Whenever she remembered Halloween these days, she couldn't help seeing herself on the Jensens' stairs, and hearing those rude voices behind her back. But she didn't want to think about that now. She didn't want Mrs. Green to be disappointed in her, and she knew her teacher would notice if she didn't pay attention. She sat up straighter in her wheelchair, and did her best to listen as Mrs. Green went on.

"We are going to learn about Kwanzaa, a holiday that celebrates African history, culture, and traditions. We are also going to learn about the traditions of a Jewish celebration called Hanukkah. We are going to talk about how people who are Hindu celebrate Divali, and how people who are Muslim celebrate Ramadan and Eid. Christmas, Hanukkah, and Divali are sometimes called Festivals of Lights, and Eid is called the Festival of Breaking the Fast. Those are five festivals celebrated with different traditions. Each one has a story."

✦✦✦

Mrs. Green stood close to the beautiful Christmas tree at the front of the class, hanging up a paper reindeer with pipe cleaners for antlers. The children were decorating the tree themselves, all of them, with crafts they were making. There were angels and dolls cut out of colored paper, and strings of popcorn. There were paper stars covered in glitter, and stars cut from foil pie plates. Right now, Anna was folding a doily into wings for the angel on top of the tree. Zoe was busy coloring a picture of the very first Christmas and the birth of Christ.

She made the Christmas star over the stable a bright yellow, and thought of the other colors she would use.

Brown for Mary's hair, and blue for her dress.

Black for Joseph's hair, and purple for his robe.

Red, green, and yellow for the Three Wise Men's robes.

Gray and black for the sheep in the stable.

Pink for the baby Jesus' rosy cheeks....

Zoe's mind went back to earlier Christmases. She remembered going into her family's small, peaceful church on Christmas Eve for a service with lots of songs from the choir. Every year, the minister handed out tiny candles for people to hold during "Silent Night," the last hymn they sang. Zoe always left with thoughts of the church dotted with all those small points of light. The memory made her smile. She couldn't wait for Christmas this year.

Each year, Zoe would sit in church and think of what it must have been like to look up in the sky and see a dazzling, bright, amazing star like the one the Wise Men had followed to find the baby Jesus. They must have been excited, shocked, happy, and scared — all at once! And how would it have felt for Jesus to be born in a manger, with hay and animals all around him? It must have been strange and uncomfortable. But it would have been warm, and Mary and Joseph were there to love him. So Zoe always ended up thinking it would have been all right.

After the Christmas Eve service, she would go home with Mom and Dad and Simon and Ella, and there would be presents and cocoa with marshmallows and….

"Ruby, be careful!"

It was Ruby's turn to water the crimson and green poinsettia on the windowsill. Zoe had looked up from her coloring just in time to see Ruby tipping the watering can too far. A puddle of water was spreading across the floor.

"Mrs. Green, look what Ruby did!" Lisa's voice shot accusingly across the room. "What a *mess!*"

"I'm not very good at watering plants," Ruby said, turning red. "I'm clumsy."

"Don't worry about it, Ruby," Mrs. Green advised. "Just wipe it up, please."

"You're not clumsy," Zoe reassured her friend. "My *dad* is clumsy. Last week he almost fell off a ladder, putting up Christmas lights outside our house!"

"Christmas lights and plants are a colorful part of the celebration," Mrs. Green said good-naturedly, as Ruby went to get paper towels and clean up the spill. "Christian homes are bright with all kinds of decorations at Christmas, and plants like our poinsettia, and mistletoe and holly, along with Christmas trees. The trees and plants help us remember that spring and summer will be back, and that nature is beautiful even when the weather is cold."

"Winter is so boring!"

"No it's not!"

"Yes it is!"

"It is *not*."

It is if you're not allowed to have snowball fights or go on toboggan rides, because your parents are always scared you'll get hurt, thought Zoe.

She had had a dream the night before, a wonderful dream. She had been swinging on a swing, so fast that she could hear the wind in her ears. Her heart had been pounding. Zoe loved the swing. She loved climbing through the air, with Simon pushing her higher, higher and higher. Mom and Dad and Anna and Ella had been like dots on the ground watching her while she *whooshed* past them.

Up, up, and up! What an adventure! She was *flying!*
Suddenly, Zoe had found herself awake.

No adventure.

But she knew she had to stop thinking that way. Feeling sorry for herself was no adventure either. It only made her miserable.

Mrs. Green was still talking.

"No arguing, boys. Winter can get cold and dark, but just when that could make us sad and lonely, a holiday like Christmas comes along to cheer us up! At Christmas, there are lots of ways to enjoy ourselves. We can sing Christmas songs, take sled rides in the snow, go skating, make snowmen and snow angels, drink hot chocolate and eat Christmas cookies...."

"My mom is already baking for Christmas," Heather said. "She always makes pies, cakes and lots of cookies — especially gingerbread cookies. And we build a gingerbread house every year!"

✖✖✖

"I've never done that, you know," Anna whispered in Zoe's ear, as she passed her desk on her way to sharpen her blue pencil.

"Done what? You make cookies all the time."

"Not *that*, silly! I've never made a gingerbread house."

Zoe's eyes grew wide. She had built so many gingerbread houses with her family. And she'd never even thought of inviting her best friend to help!

Chapter Four
THE INTRUDER

"Simon, Anna, William, Zoe, if you don't stop eating gumdrops and Smarties there won't be any left for the gingerbread houses."

"Sorry, Mrs. Dempsey," Anna said, carefully covering her mouth, since it was full of candy. "We won't eat anymore."

"Speak for yourself," Simon teased, still chewing, trying not to spit anything out. William laughed.

"We'll *try* not to eat anymore," Zoe promised.

"Well, how about you all go out in the backyard, away from the candies, and play with Ella while there's still some light out there? I'll call you when the gingerbread is cool. The way you're going, you'll be too full to even look at your gingerbread houses when they're ready!"

"Well…." William was gazing at the gumdrops, which he couldn't quite reach.

"Aw, *Mom*," complained Simon.

"Come on, it'll be fun," Zoe urged. "Ella's out there already, having her 'dog time.'" Ella got some free time every day as a break from being "on duty" and helping Zoe. "She always waits for me to come out and play with her. Let's go!"

↖↖↖

Zoe saw Rufus first.

She crossed the porch ahead of everyone else, with Anna close behind her. She looked down the wheelchair ramp toward Ella's favorite side of the house, and began to call her.

"El —" *Oh!*

It was unmistakably the skunk — furry and black with a broad white stripe down his back. He had been regarding the backyard from a spot halfway up the ramp. He reacted to Zoe's voice with the confidence of a prince, calmly turning toward her. They locked eyes, and Zoe wished desperately that she hadn't said anything at all. But it was too late.

It wouldn't have mattered anyway.

Ella was always aware of Zoe's presence, whether Zoe spoke or not. The dog had heard her the moment she came out of the house. She always, *always* came when Zoe appeared.

So there was no way around it. Ella was on her way to Zoe — and Rufus was between the two of them.

By now, everyone else had come out of the house too. They had joined Anna in stunned silence behind Zoe. They were in time to see Ella trot around the corner of the house and look up the ramp at Zoe.

Rufus whirled to face this new threat, and now he didn't look so calm.

He stomped his paws deliberately, in warning. He wasn't going to run away. He didn't have to.

All Zoe could think of in that moment were her father's words to Simon the week before: *Getting sprayed by a skunk is no joke.*

She froze. She sat there like a statue, like an icicle.

She did nothing.

As for Ella, she stopped in her tracks, puzzled. What was she supposed to do? She needed to get to Zoe. And here was Rufus, right in the way.

But taking care of Zoe was Ella's job. She had no choice.

She started up the ramp, uncertain but determined

— focusing on Zoe, focusing on her goal. She would do her job, for better or worse.

"Oh, *no*, Ella," Zoe whispered.

The children could only stand there and watch as Rufus stomped menacingly one more time, turned his back on Ella, looked directly at her over his shoulder, raised his tail, and sprayed....

Eew! What a *horrible* smell!

Rufus calmly hopped through the railing and off the ramp, heading for the nearest bushes. Poor Ella stiffened, looking shocked and hurt and indignant. All the children backed away from the stinking dog, gagging and holding their noses, except for Zoe and Anna.

Zoe held her arms out and Ella ran to her, blinking and whimpering. She hurled herself at Zoe and rubbed her face in Zoe's lap, trying to wipe off that horrid smell. And the noises she made! Crying, moaning, almost shrieking!

Zoe's mother appeared in the doorway and clapped a hand over her nose.

"Zoe, Anna! Everybody!" she shouted. *"Get away from Ella!! You're all going to stink!"*

Anna obeyed her, but Zoe shot her mother a look at once scared and stubborn. "I'm not leaving my dog alone. She's hurt and she's afraid!"

"Come in here! You'll ruin your clothes!"

"No!"

Mrs. Dempsey looked at the two of them. She saw Ella's face buried in her daughter's lap, as the dog desperately searched for comfort. She saw Zoe stroking her dog and murmuring gentle, loving words to calm her.

She gave in and threw her hands in the air. "I don't know what to do. I don't know where to start!"

By then, Zoe's dad had heard the commotion. He came outside and saw the other kids huddled on the porch, holding their noses. "What in the world happened?" he asked.

With that, everyone was talking at once.

"How could an animal as cute as Rufus smell so *gross*?" Anna wondered.

"He's not really named Rufus," Simon pointed out. "Old Mr. Hollingsworth just called him that because he couldn't see him well enough to know he was a skunk and not a stray cat!"

"Poor Ella. Look at her! Boy, does she stink!" William exclaimed.

"What about Zoe? Ella's been rubbing up against her!" said Anna, who was feeling a little guilty that she hadn't stayed with Zoe.

"I don't believe this. That dog's going to smell *forever!*"

"Yuck! Gross! It's disgusting!"

"What are we going to *do*?"

Then Zoe's voice rang out, clear and strong, over the confusion. "Simon! Go and find Nalini! Now!"

Chapter Five

TAKING CHARGE

Simon was back almost at once, with a large paper bag in his arms, and with Ruby and Nalini right behind him. Ruby was always surprised by how much power Nalini had when she needed it. *She's a problem-solver, that's for sure*, the girl thought.

"Thanks for coming," Zoe's mother said gratefully.

"We don't know what to do, and we don't have enough tomato juice to wash this big dog."

"Rubbish! You don't need tomato juice," Nalini exclaimed. "What works is liquid soap, baking soda, peroxide. It's all in the bag. Ella won't like this, but if you do it my way, she'll smell like sunshine in no time."

↟↟↟

Nalini took one look at all the anxious faces in the backyard, and took charge. "Let me just catch my breath. *Oof!* Now — Zoe, you need to get cleaned up before you even think of helping your dog. You *both* smell like the wrong end of Rufus! Go with Anna, get washed and put some old clothes on."

"But — " Zoe began to protest. Nalini stopped her with a stern look. "Let us take care of cleaning up Ella, okay? Tell her to *stay*, and you go, please. Now!"

With a heavy heart, Zoe did as she was told. Ella was confused, but she understood that Zoe knew best. The dog whimpered and whined, but she didn't try to follow. Before Zoe rolled her wheelchair indoors, though, she made a firm announcement.

"Before I leave Ella for even two minutes, you all have to promise me that you won't set up her bath outside. I don't care how she smells; it's too cold to wash her out here." She looked around at everyone. "Do you *promise?*"

"Where are we going to do it, then? The whole house will smell if we bring her inside," Nalini pointed out.

"Take her through the garage to the laundry room. We'll do it in there," Zoe said. "And one more thing. You can set up her bath, but you have to wait for me to come and wash her. She's *my* dog, and she's so scared and mixed up. You can't do it without me. It's not fair."

Zoe's mother and Nalini thought about this for a long moment. Finally, they decided she was right. "Okay, you have our word," her mother assured her. "Now go and get clean. We'll set everything up, but we won't give her the bath until you're there."

As Zoe left with Anna, they could hear Nalini behind them, straightening out the confusion. Everyone was being given a job to do.

★★★

"Thanks for helping, Anna. I can't get ready so fast by myself, and I really want to get back to Ella. She's so upset! I really hope that bath works!"

"Don't worry, Nalini's done this before. Remember that time Mustang got sprayed? But I'm glad you told them not to start the bath without you. They *can't* do it without you. Ella would be too scared. She needs you there."

Zoe felt her throat close, and suddenly tears burned the back of her eyes. "It's my fault!"

Anna stared at her best friend, and put her arm around her. "*What's* your fault?"

"This whole thing!" Zoe cried. "Ella and I are supposed to take care of *each other*. I take care of her, and she takes care of me. Anytime I need her, she's there for me. If I had been taking care of *her*, watching out for her, she wouldn't have gotten sprayed. When Aunt Jessica's dog Oscar almost got sprayed, she picked him up and put him inside and shut the door just in time...she acted really *fast*, and nothing bad happened to Oscar. If I had acted fast instead of freezing up, sitting there like a lump, Ella would be okay."

"But we were all there and we all froze up. It wasn't just you! And don't forget, Oscar is little. He's easy to rescue. He fits in your aunt's lap. Ella can only get her *head* in your lap. So how could anybody just pick her up and save her? Anyway, animals get sprayed by skunks all the time. Even Mustang, and Nalini takes really good care of him."

"Yeah...," Zoe said hesitantly. "But Ella came straight to me when I started to call her. She didn't even try to protect herself. She trusted me to protect her. And I let her down."

Now Anna looked shocked. "Of course you protected her! You figured out what to do. You sent Simon to Nalini's right away. You stood up for Ella and made sure her bath would be in the laundry room, not out in the cold. Now let's go and get Ella washed and clean again!"

Zoe sighed and then smiled a little. "Okay. But I don't think one bath is going to fix that stink. She'll need a lot of baths, and she's going to hate every minute of every one."

It was strange, because Ella loved water. She'd run through the sprinkler in summer, and she'd swim with Zoe at the cottage. But as soon as anyone came near her with shampoo, her eyes said *please, no*, her tail went between her legs, and she was *miserable*.

Anna giggled. "Look on the bright side."

"There's a bright side?"

"Sure," Anna answered. "We'll never forget the first time we made gingerbread together, will we?"

❤❤❤

The minute Zoe arrived in the laundry room, Ella left Simon and William, who had been playing quietly with her, and came bounding over. But her joy didn't last long.

"We're ready, Zoe!" her mother told her. "We need to get Ella in the laundry tub, please."

Zoe's dad had put a wooden chair beside the tub, to help Ella climb up. He'd put a towel on the bottom of the tub so it wouldn't be slippery. Now they just needed the dog.

"Please, Ella, come on, be a good girl. That's it, get in the tub. That's a good dog!" Zoe coaxed.

Ella clearly knew that this bath was going to be a big deal. She took one look at the laundry tub and tried to back away. But she loved Zoe and wanted to please her. And maybe she understood that the bath had something to do with getting rid of the horrible smell on her fur. Maybe she knew that it was worth having a bath.

But she didn't have to be happy about it!

Once Ella was inside the tub — with the aid of the chair and a boost from Zoe's dad — she stood looking mournful as Zoe positioned herself in front of her and held her head gently but firmly. It wasn't because Ella could escape very far — all the doors were closed. But no one wanted to have to get her back into that tub again.

Zoe's mom removed Ella's collar and held it at arm's length, wrinkling her nose. "We'll have to deal with this later," she commented. "What a wretched smell! I'm glad Ella wasn't wearing her harness when Rufus came along."

Zoe spoke soothingly to the dog while Nalini and her mother worked. Ella's sad eyes were almost too much for Zoe to handle, but this had to be done. Once they rubbed Nalini's mixture into her fur, Ella was covered in soapy suds, white lather and bubbles.

"She looks more like a sheep!" Zoe's mother kidded.

Zoe wanted to be annoyed with her mother. How dare she poke fun at the poor dog! But looking at Ella, she had a strong urge to laugh herself. She managed not to, but her mother and Nalini and even Anna were beginning to giggle.

Was it possible for a furry brown dog to turn pink? Ella looked positively tragic, and that was enough to set Zoe straight. "Ella *hates* being laughed at! Everybody stop! Let's just get this done, please," she pleaded.

They scrubbed more lather into Ella's fur, rinsed her off, added more soap, then scrubbed and rinsed, and scrubbed and rinsed again. By the time Ella was rinsed for the last time, everyone was very tired and sopping wet.

"Okay," Nalini finally announced. "I think she can come out now."

Ella didn't wait to be asked. She leapt out of the tub, bounced off the floor, and launched herself into Zoe's arms. Zoe hugged her close, though they were both soaking. As soon as Zoe let Ella go, the dog got down, braced her four feet, and shook purposefully from head to tail. Water flew in all directions.

"It's raining in here!" Zoe laughed and dried her dog's fur with a soft, clean towel while Ella licked her face all over.

"I think she's attached to you for life," Anna whispered to Zoe.

That suited Zoe just fine.

Chapter Six

KWANZAA GIFTS

"Zoe, do you *mind*?"

"What? I didn't do anything."

"I'm trying to draw. I hate it when you watch me like that!"

Zoe shrank back from peering over Simon's shoulder and sipped her orange juice, shooting him a couple of hurt looks.

"Zoe, leave your brother alone," Dad warned, as he buttered his toast. "He's trying to finish his art assignment. He has to hand it in this morning. Don't bug him when he's working, okay?"

"I'm not bugging him."

"She's bugging me," Simon confirmed, as he carefully

shaded the wings of the huge hawk on the page. Just then, the phone rang.

"I'll get it!" Mom called from the hall.

Zoe sat quietly disappointed — very much like Ella, who lay under the kitchen table hoping for toast crumbs. Zoe picked up her juice again and sneaked a sideways glance at the hawk's strong feet, and then his hooked beak and claws. His piercing yellow eyes stared at her from the paper.

"The puppies were born this morning!" Mom's voice rang out with the news. "There are five girls and four boys," she announced excitedly.

Aunt Beth's puppies! Zoe wanted to cheer. "I want to talk to her!" she bellowed, reaching to put down her glass.

"Not so fast," Dad objected. "Aunt Beth can wait. Finish your —"

It was too late. In her rush, Zoe misjudged as she put down her glass. It hit the edge of her plate, and seemed to leap from her hand. Suddenly, Simon's drawing was drenched in orange juice! He jumped back to avoid the spreading flood.

Zoe wailed, "Noooo!"

"Zoeeeee!" Simon shrieked.

It was chaos. Startled, Ella barked and jumped up so fast that the table rocked. Dad leapt to save Simon's pencil box, and Mom rushed into the room and ran to help clean up.

Zoe looked at the floor. She felt so sick that she wanted to disappear. She knew the drawing was ruined.

Simon stared at her, and his eyes narrowed. "You did it on purpose," he accused her.

She could barely find her voice. "No. I…I was just trying to…."

"You were just trying to get back at me because I didn't let you watch me. You were mad because you didn't get your way. You're *spoiled*."

"Simon, stop," Dad said firmly.

"Simon, you know that's not true," Mom added. "Zoe didn't mean it. It was an accident."

"No it wasn't, Mom. You weren't even here!"

✦✦✦

Happy Kwanzaa! That was the first thing Zoe read in class after recess. It was on a big banner that hung at the front. On the wall beside the blackboard was a huge poster, too, with words listed from top to bottom in big, fancy letters. Zoe read: *Unity, Self-determination, Teamwork and Responsibility, Co-operation, Purpose, Creativity,* and, last, *Faith*.

"Happy Kwanzaa!" Mrs. Green was saying to each of them — including Ella — as they came back in from the schoolyard.

It was good to see her teacher treating Ella just as she always did. Kids had been wrinkling their noses at the dog all day. "She smells funny!" they whispered. After telling over and over what had happened with Rufus on Thursday, Zoe just ignored the talk. She didn't want to explain anymore. She was already feeling low. That was the last thing she needed.

"You look so upset. Never mind her," Anna told Zoe, as the girls saw Lisa's disgusted face. Lisa was showing off, holding her nose whenever she saw Zoe and Ella. "Let's talk about something else. What's up with Simon today? He didn't even say hi to me this morning."

Oh great, Zoe thought. "I'll tell you later," she said.

When everyone was back in class, Mrs. Green clapped her hands for attention. "Everyone get settled, please," she called out.

Zoe had never seen her teacher dressed as beautifully as she was today. Tied around her head like a turban was a large, bright red, black, and green scarf. Her blouse and long skirt were a cheery yellow, and at her waist was a wide black belt. Green bracelets jangled on her arms, and she wore green hoop earrings to match.

"Mrs. Green, what's going on today? What's Kwanzaa?" Zoe asked.

"Why are there *corncobs* on our desks?" Anna held hers up.

"You'll find out as soon as everyone sits and quiets down," promised the teacher.

Zoe looked around the room to see what else hadn't been there before recess. There was a table against the far wall, covered in a green, red, and black striped cloth with a placemat on it. On top of the placemat sat a wooden candleholder with seven candles — three red, three green, and a black one in the middle. A big straw basket full of fruit — apples, oranges, bananas, a mango, a coconut, and a pineapple — was on the table too.

Mrs. Green pulled a drum out from behind her desk and started to play, hitting it steadily with her palms. As the beat spread through the room, the talking stopped, and soon the only sound was the drum's rhythm.

As it died down, the teacher's voice took over, strong and clear.

"Kwanzaa is a celebration of freedom. Today, you'll see a bit of what that celebration is like. There are dried corncobs on your desks. In the Kwanzaa tradition, each of the corncobs stands for one child in the celebration. Children — that means you — make us hopeful, and Kwanzaa is about hope, too."

"Boys!" she suddenly called out. Zoe turned to find out what the commotion was about, and she saw Peter and Mario bopping each other's heads with the corncobs. "The corncobs are *not* for swatting each other! Stop that!"

"We're just joking around," Mario protested, trying to stop giggling.

"Put those down and don't pick them up unless you're asked. Do I make myself clear?"

"Sorry," Mario said.

"That's better. Don't let me see that again. Now, back to what I was saying before you started beating yourselves up. Kwanzaa is a festival that lasts for seven days, and it honors African history and traditions. During Kwanzaa, people like me, who have an African background but live far away from Africa, spend time remembering what makes us unique, learning from the past, and looking forward to the future. We celebrate our talents, and what is good within ourselves and within all people."

"The word 'Kwanzaa' means "first fruits" in an African language called Swahili. The festival celebrates the gathering of food, and it's a time to think about unity and courage. Kwanzaa may remind you of Thanksgiving. On that table over there, you see the basket of fruit. It helps us remember that the Earth grows the food we need, and communities of people gather and eat it. Food brings us together. The placemat under the basket stands for the beginnings, or roots, of African culture. And the candles are an important part of the tradition, too. Every home celebrating Kwanzaa has a table decorated like this."

"Are we gonna get to have Kwanzaa food?" Paul asked.

"Not today. We'll talk about that later. Learning about the festivals is not just about eating good food. Right now, we're learning what makes Kwanzaa special. When black people were captured and brought here from Africa hundreds of years ago against their will, they were treated very badly. They were not allowed to go to school, and they were forced to work terribly hard. They were treated as if they weren't really people, just because their skin was dark."

"No school? That would rock!" Adam interrupted.

"Are you *stupid?*" blurted Zoe. "How would you feel if you could never read your comic books again?"

"*Zoe!*" Mrs. Green sounded shocked. "We don't call people names in this class. You know better than that."

"I didn't call him stupid. I asked him if he *was* stupid," Zoe pointed out.

"That doesn't matter. The problem is that you were rude. You know better than that, too. One more wisecrack and you'll be out in the hall. Understood?"

Zoe turned redder than a ripe strawberry. "Yes, Mrs. Green."

The teacher continued. "Adam, you need to understand that missing school because you went on a vacation, or because you caught a cold, is nothing like being *forced* to miss out on any schooling at all. When they were used as slaves, these people from Africa lived a very harsh life. They had no rights and no freedom! Their stories, traditions and history were lost. But they were determined to begin new traditions and tell new stories. They dreamed of freedom, talking and singing about it as they worked and whenever they could gather. Kwanzaa is important because it helps their descendants to celebrate who we are now, to honor others who inspire us, and to remember people who made a difference, who protected us when we didn't have rights, and worked to change things so that we have equal rights today. Kwanzaa is a happy time when we learn from the past, but it is also a time when we promise to be good to ourselves and honor each other. It's a time to sing, dance, tell stories, and be proud and joyful about all the things we are doing, all the things we've done, and everything we can do."

I was unfair to Adam, Zoe admitted to herself. *Even though what he said really bugged me, I shouldn't have talked to him like that.*

"And each day, at the end of the celebration," Mrs. Green went on, "everyone calls out, 'Let's pull together!' Everyone try that."

"Let's pull together," they mumbled.

"You sound like you're asleep," Mrs. Green said. "Let's try again, on the count of three. One…two…three…."

"*Let's pull together!*" they chorused.

What's the matter with me today? Zoe wondered. *I was rude this morning too. If I'd left Simon alone with his art stuff, nothing bad would've happened.* The thought suddenly popped into Zoe's head as she joined in, and she knew it was true. Guilt dropped into her stomach like a rock.

That was when she decided.

She would explain things to Simon. She would make it all right again.

ᐱᐱᐱ

"So Kwanzaa is about how things got better for black people?" asked Anna.

"You're right, it is," Mrs. Green said. "And this celebration was created not too long ago, in 1967."

"That was *ages* ago!" Lisa exclaimed.

Mrs. Green laughed. "That was before any of you

were born, but not a very long time before. Kwanzaa was created by an African-American man named Dr. Maulana Karenga. He was one of the people who worked to give black people the same rights as everyone else. The celebration is based on the seven principles on that poster over there, and we think of a different principle on each day of Kwanzaa." She pointed to the poster. "Let's say them together. Repeat after me...."

✦✦✦

"Mrs. Green, I know Kwanzaa is about more than food," Heather said shyly after that, "but we're going to have food, right?"

Everyone laughed, including Mrs. Green. "Yes, later this week there will be food, I promise," she said. "We'll have our own Kwanzaa feast here, just like the one that takes place in the evening of the sixth day of the celebration. There will be chicken and dumplings, candied sweet potatoes, African peanut chicken, banana bread, beans and rice, fruit salad, even Jamaican carrot juice. And at the end of today, I will have a surprise announcement for you."

"Yuck, *carrot* juice? Gross!" Ruby couldn't help interrupting.

"Don't say that until you've tried it," the teacher advised. "It's delicious. You'll see."

There was a chorus of begging. "Tell us about our surprise now! *Pleeease?*"

"If I told you now, it wouldn't be a surprise, would it?"

"Yes it will! It will! Tell us!"

"Be patient," Mrs. Green said. "But I'll give you a hint, and let's see if you can guess. On the sixth day of Kwanzaa, we exchange gifts."

"We're getting presents!" Zoe cried.

"Yes, you guessed it," Mrs. Green agreed. "You're all going to make presents for each other, and you won't know who made yours until we exchange them. Tomorrow, each of us — including me — will write our names on pieces of paper and put the pieces in a hat. Then I'll call you to the front of the room one by one. You're going to close your eyes tight and reach into the hat to pick out a piece of paper with the name of the person you will make a gift for. Does anyone have any questions?"

"Can we tell the person?"

"No, I just told you that you keep that part a secret until next week. That's when we will all give our gifts. And that's when we'll have our Kwanzaa feast."

"Simon, I'm sorry I wrecked your drawing."

No answer.

Zoe sat in her brother's bedroom doorway and watched him reading his comic book, flopped on his bed.

"I *said* I'm sorry about your drawing."

"I heard you," he grunted, without looking at her.

Zoe took a deep breath. "I *am* sorry, but it was an accident."

Silence.

"I don't mean to make you mad when I watch you draw. But I love the way you draw, and I love birds. I love to watch them zipping through the trees, or gliding high in the sky, so fast and so free. Remember how great it was when we had Jade? Of course, Ella's better than a parakeet, but still — I really miss that little bird. That's why I couldn't help watching you do your drawing. And I didn't spill my juice on purpose. I was excited about the puppies, and —"

"This isn't about you!" Simon shot back. "That drawing was almost done, and Mr. Westover was going to enter it in that art competition for me! Now I have to start all over again, and it's *your* fault!"

"Simon, listen, I —"

"No! For once it isn't your turn! You get all Mom and Dad's attention, all the time! They always take your

49

side! It's always 'be nice to Zoe' or 'it's hard for Zoe.' Well, I have news for you: it's hard for Simon, too!"

Zoe stared at him, open-mouthed.

"Get out of my room!"

✗✗✗

"Simon, apologize to your sister right now. You have no right to speak to her that way."

Mom stood behind Zoe with a basket of laundry in her hands. "Simon Christopher Dempsey, I'm waiting."

Zoe found her voice. "No, Mom. He's allowed to be mad at me. If I were him, I'd be mad too. I shouldn't have butted in when he was trying to finish his project this morning. And he's right. I do get a lot of attention.

"But Simon," she continued, "when I get extra attention, it's because Mom or Dad is working with me on my physio exercises, or because I called for help with something. When you get time with Dad, you ride your bikes or go hiking or rollerblading or play hockey. You get to have fun! Physio isn't fun!"

"Zoe," Mom put in, "we're not always doing physio. We have fun. We go to the movies, go shopping, go...."

"I didn't say we never have fun, Mom," Zoe said quickly. "I'm talking about the *extra* time I get, that Simon doesn't. He thinks I'm spoiled. But that's okay. He doesn't have to understand. Don't yell at him, it isn't fair."

With that, Zoe wheeled herself away.

🗲🗲🗲

The next day, Zoe held the folded piece of paper that she had just pulled out of the hat. Half of her really wanted to see whose name was written on the inside. The other half dreaded finding out. What gift would she make? She had no ideas at all.

You can't decide what to make if you don't know who you're making it for, she told herself.

"Whose name have you got?" Ruby whispered.

"We're not supposed to tell," Zoe reminded her friend. It was easier than explaining why she hadn't looked yet.

This is nuts, she thought.

When Ruby walked away, looking disappointed, Zoe quickly unfolded her piece of paper, and gasped.

🗲🗲🗲

"You should be proud," Dad told Zoe, as they set the dinner table together. "It's a pretty important job to make a gift for your teacher."

51

"Yeah, but it has to be really *good* now. Everyone in class will want to know what Mrs. Green gets."

"You're supposed to do your best job no matter who you're making the gift for," Dad reminded her.

Zoe rolled her eyes. "I *know* that," she said, sighing.

"Zoe, you write your own poems all the time," Mom reminded her, as she brought the tuna casserole to the table.

"So?"

"Well, you could write one for Mrs. Green, and then read it to the class. That could be her present. She would love it!"

"You expect me to read my poem in front of the whole class? Are you *joking*?"

"Why not? You're good at poetry, and it doesn't have to be a long poem. You can do it. It's perfect."

"No it's not," Zoe said.

But she began to think. Mom's words rang in her ears. *You're good at poetry.*

✦✦✦

Zoe's hands shook as she held her poem in her hands. *You're going to do this*, she told herself. *You're going to read it out loud. It's her present.*

Still, the first two lines came out almost in a whisper.

"Kwanzaa tells me
That we should all be free."

Lisa was snickering at her. Zoe looked away and closed her eyes for a minute. She saw Anna in her mind, saying, *Never mind her.* So Zoe opened her eyes again and kept going, her voice much louder.

"It's a big celebration
Of courage and tradition.
We must honor what is past
And make the lesson last.
So Adam, Ruby, Heather —
Let's all pull together!"

She'd done it! Zoe finished and didn't even look at Lisa. Mrs. Green was beaming!

She came over and gave Zoe a big hug. "Thank-you. That was a beautiful poem, and you did a great job making us think of what Kwanzaa celebrates!"

It was the best thank-you ever!

✦✦✦

"Zoe, this is your present. And I liked your poem," Samir said shyly.

"Thanks," she said, swallowing a mouthful of peanut chicken and sweet potatoes, and smiling at him. She didn't know Samir very well, so when she looked down and saw what he'd made for her, she was very surprised.

And she laughed! She laughed so hard that tears came to her eyes. It was perfect!

It was a cartoon, a picture of Ella in Zoe's wheelchair, sitting happily with her pink tongue lolling out excitedly. And in the cartoon, Zoe was standing behind the wheelchair, pushing it.

There was a cartoon bubble right over Ella's head, to show what she was thinking: "Now *this* is more like it!"

"Look, Ella!" Zoe exclaimed. "Look at us! Isn't this funny? Look at what Samir drew for us!"

Ella wagged her tail.

✦✦✦

Simon's new drawing was on the fridge when Zoe got home from school that night. When she saw it, her eyes grew wide.

There were birds, so many birds — hundreds it seemed — all taking off together from the branches of a huge tree. She wanted to congratulate him on the drawing, to ask him if Mr. Westover would enter this one in the contest instead of the one she had ruined. But she was nervous. What if Simon was still mad at her?

There was only one way to find out.

Even though his bedroom door was open, she knocked on it this time.

He looked up from his math notebook. "Hi," he said.

"Hi." All of a sudden, Zoe didn't know what to say. *You have to say something*, she thought.

"I saw your new drawing. It's really good."

"Thanks. I…I think I like this one even better."

"That's good…Okay, well…see you later," Zoe said, turning to go.

"Zoe?" Simon called.

"Yeah?"

"Can you come here for a minute?"

"Why?"

"I wanna show you something."

Puzzled, Zoe pushed herself toward her brother's desk, with Ella following behind. *Maybe he's still mad at me after all*, she couldn't help worrying. *Maybe he's going to show me the old picture with sticky orange juice all over it, and start yelling at me again.* Part of her wanted to turn and go, but she didn't.

When Zoe reached him, though, Simon didn't yell. He tore a clean page out of his notebook and picked up a sharp pencil. "Okay, now watch what I do," he told her. "If you want to draw a bird, here's how you start...."

Chapter Seven
THE
HANUKKAH CANDLE

One week and three more baths later, Ella smelled like her usual self again.

Anna and Zoe were on the bus with Ella and Mrs. Myers, Anna's mother. The girls could hardly sit still. They were on the way from school to Anna's house to celebrate the first night of Hanukkah, the Jewish Festival of Lights. But Anna and Zoe were having trouble thinking only about Hanukkah. Aunt Beth was trying to find homes for all the pups in her new litter. Zoe and Anna had visited them the day before, and Anna wanted one for her own, very, very badly.

"I love the way all the puppies were playing on that blanket. The one I want is *soooo* cute, Zoe! It's the one that was rolling over and running all the time, the black one. I'm going to call her Cinder. It'll be perfect, Zoe! My Cinder and your Ella! Cinderella!" Both girls giggled.

"It'll be so much fun!" Zoe exclaimed. "We'll teach her to sit and fetch and...."

"Okay, girls, that's enough daydreaming. You can think about puppies later. For now, we should be thinking about Hanukkah. The celebration begins tonight, after all."

Anna and Zoe tried to sit still and think of the miracle of Hanukkah. Thousands of years ago, in Jerusalem, a lamp with sacred oil in it had burned in a Jewish temple for eight whole days — even though the lamp had only enough oil to burn for one day! The miracle of the lamp was even more special because it had happened after the temple was nearly ruined, and people had worked long and hard to save it.

The girls knew Hanukkah was amazing, and important to remember. But whenever they closed their eyes, they didn't see a lamp or a temple. They saw nine adorable, squirming puppies!

All was quiet until the bus hit a bump and the girls were jolted in their seats.

"Ouch!"

"Yikes!"

Zoe looked around to see what had happened. That was when she saw him.

"Anna, isn't that Samir sitting by himself over there?"

"I think so. I wonder where Adam is. That's weird. They're always together. "

Like us, Zoe thought. "I'm gonna call him over."

"He looks sad. Maybe he wants to be by himself."

"He looks lonely," Zoe countered, catching Samir's attention with a big wave. At the next bus stop, he made his way toward them.

"Hey guys." His smile was wobbly.

Samir sat beside Zoe and leaned back. "Can I pet Ella?"

Zoe looked down at her dog. Ella had her special harness on, the one she wore when she had to concentrate on helping Zoe. Seeing the harness gave people the message not to distract the dog by talking to her or petting her. Ella had to focus on Zoe even more when they were out, so strangers needed this warning that the dog was busy.

But Samir was not a stranger. And he looked so sad.

"Sure. Go ahead." Zoe kept her voice light, knowing

that Ella would help him feel better. *Something is wrong,* she thought.

"How is your mom, Samir?" Mrs. Myers asked.

"She's fine. She's cooking tons of food for me to bring to school for the Eid feast day. She keeps kicking me out of the kitchen so I don't eat everything!"

"Say hello to her for me, please."

"Okay."

"If Simon were here, he would tell you to say hi to Adam," Zoe ventured. "Where is Adam, anyway?"

"I don't want to talk about Adam," Samir snapped.

Anna shot Zoe a look. *Wrong move,* it said.

"Are you all right, kiddo?" Mrs. Myers asked Samir. "You seem awfully quiet today,"

"Yeah, I'm okay, I guess."

But Samir got off the bus at the next stop, without saying another word.

✄✄✄

In just a few minutes, they would light the first Hanukkah candle in the Myers' menorah — a special, large candle-holder with space for nine candles. Jewish people lit the candles bit by bit — one today, the first day of Hanukkah, two tomorrow, the second day, and so on, until all eight were burning. This was to remind them of the miracle of the Hanukkah lamp.

Zoe loved Hanukkah. She loved gathering around the menorah and lighting it right after the sun went down. She loved playing dreidel — a game that had been around for thousands of years, and had helped keep the Jewish faith, customs, and traditions strong.

✦✦✦

"I wish we were celebrating Hanukkah in Jerusalem," Anna said, as they ate dinner together a little later. "We haven't been there since before Papa died." Her voice quivered just a little.

"Maybe we will be there next year," Anna's mother said, a touch of sadness in her voice.

"What's Hanukkah like in Jerusalem?" Zoe wanted to know, eager to change the subject. She hated to see people she loved feeling sad.

"Oh, it's so much fun!" Anna's face brightened. "At the beginning of Hanukkah there is a huge torch relay race, and before it starts there is a big bonfire that the runners use to light their torches. Lots and lots of people come to watch and cheer as the runners race and pass their torches on to other runners. At the end of the race, a rabbi lights a giant menorah and blesses the Hanukkah celebrations. It's amazing! All over Jerusalem, there are menorahs shining. It's so beautiful! I wish you could see it."

"Now, *that* would be an adventure!" Zoe exclaimed.

"What is it with you and adventures lately?" Anna sounded curious.

"Adventures are important," Zoe answered. *But I wonder if I'll ever get to have one...a real one...*she thought.

If she did, she knew Anna would be with her. Unless....

Zoe couldn't get Samir's hurt voice out of her mind. *I don't want to talk about Adam,* he had said. But Samir and Adam were best friends. Everyone knew that. What had happened? Could it ever happen to her and Anna?

"Zoe, aren't you hungry?" Anna's mother asked gently. "You haven't touched your dinner."

"Oh, yes, Mrs. Myers, I love Hanukkah food," Zoe said quickly. "I was just...thinking, that's all."

No more worrying, she told herself firmly. She concentrated on eating her food. It was so good that she could barely decide where to start. Anna's mother had made a special salad with cucumber — Zoe's favorite — and tomatoes, parsley, and green onions. There was other great food too — roast chicken, green beans, carrots, and honey cake. And there was applesauce to eat with the potato latkes — the best potato pancakes Zoe had ever tasted! Even Ella, snoozing under the table, gobbled up the bits of latke that Zoe gave her as a very special treat.

For a while — just a little while — Zoe didn't even think about adventures.

When their plates were empty, Mrs. Myers went to get the dessert. "I know this will remind you of Jerusalem, Anna," she said, as she brought in a big dish of exactly what the girls were hoping for: warm jelly doughnuts called *sufganiyot* in Hebrew.

"Enjoy them, girls. I waited in a long line at the bakery to get these. I think *everybody* wants them during Hanukkah!"

Zoe wished she could see Hanukkah in Jerusalem. Right now, though, celebrating here with this family was wonderful! She imagined all the menorahs in the world shining warmly.

She was especially happy because Anna's mother had chosen her to light the first candle that night, and helped keep her hand steady while she did it. It was an honor to play such an important part in this tradition. It made Zoe glow inside, like the flame she had lit.

Chapter Eight
CHEATED!

And then, suddenly, things began to go wrong at school.

It started when the class played dreidel, on one of the days they learned about Hanukkah.

When Mrs. Green told the class that they were about to break into pairs and play the game, Zoe looked for Anna to be her partner. They both had lots of practice at dreidel.

But Anna's desk was empty. For a moment, Zoe had forgotten that her friend was home that day, because she had a cold.

Zoe looked down at Ella sitting beside her. This was another one of those times when her beautiful dog couldn't do anything to help; she couldn't be her partner in the game. Everyone else in the class was finding a partner fast. On every table Zoe looked at, there was a top spinning, with people playing and laughing.

Zoe thought of the last time she and Anna had played. Chocolate coins wrapped in gold paper had been piled in the middle of Anna's kitchen table, and they had had a small pile of chocolate coins for themselves, too. They had played by spinning a top marked with Hebrew symbols, instead of throwing dice marked with dots.

Zoe and Anna had taken turns spinning the top, to see which symbol came up when it landed. The symbols told them what to do with the coins. Zoe might be allowed to add all the coins in the center of the table to her own pile, or to take just half of them. She might have to put all her own coins into the pile in the middle. Or she might lose a turn, giving Anna two turns in a row. The winner of the game was the player who ended up with all the chocolate coins. In that last game with Anna, Zoe had won. But would she win today?

Zoe looked around the class again. It seemed that everyone else was already playing. Would she even find a partner, or would she not play at all? She was all by herself — except for Ella, of course.

"Do you need a partner, Zoe?"

Zoe looked up, surprised to see Lisa standing there with her bouncy red curls. Lisa had never been very nice to her.

"Do you want to play dreidel with me?" Lisa asked.

"All right," Zoe said. *This could be my only chance to play today,* she thought.

"Here, I can spin the top for you," Lisa said, when it was Zoe's turn.

"I can do that myself," Zoe said, but Lisa had already spun the top for her. When it stopped, Zoe saw the symbol meaning that she could take half the chocolate coins from the center of the desk and add them to her own pile.

But before she could reach for the extra coins, Lisa snatched them. "That symbol means *I* get extra," she crowed.

Zoe could hardly believe it! Did Lisa really think she didn't understand what the symbol meant? Why was Lisa telling such a lie? She was so astonished that she didn't even argue.

✗✗✗

Somehow, Zoe managed to get through the rest of the game of dreidel, but for the rest of the day she could not pay attention. She thought and thought about the game and the sick feeling in her stomach when Lisa took all those chocolate coins that didn't belong to her. Zoe was sad and upset. Lisa had won the game, but she had cheated — not just once, but again and again. Worse yet, she had acted as if Zoe couldn't possibly understand the rules of the game.

It wasn't losing that bothered Zoe so much. It was the feeling that Lisa thought she wasn't smart. It was the feeling that Lisa only thought that because Zoe needed a wheelchair. The fact that Zoe used a wheelchair to move around, and had a dog to help her, didn't mean she couldn't think for herself!

But if Zoe could think for herself, why hadn't she told Mrs. Green that Lisa was cheating? Why hadn't she at least stood up for herself? Why hadn't she refused to play with Lisa anymore, once she knew that Lisa was cheating, and once she knew that Lisa thought she wasn't smart enough to know about it? Why hadn't Zoe said something to show Lisa how wrong she was?

Zoe had been scared, that was why. She'd been surprised. She'd known that Lisa wasn't her friend, but she hadn't known that Lisa thought she was helpless. She hadn't known that at all.

Zoe glanced at Lisa, who was sitting at her desk with

her head of red curls tilted toward the girl next to her. Lisa was whispering something in the girl's ear. They both giggled…and then Lisa looked over her shoulder at Zoe, and giggled again!

Zoe fought back tears. She missed Anna more than ever. And she was beginning to get angry. She was beginning to get very, *very* angry!

✦✦✦

Zoe didn't say much at home that night. Who would understand, anyway? Mom and Dad wouldn't know how it felt for people to think they weren't smart. Everyone knew how smart they were.

Simon wouldn't understand either. He would just tease her.

She didn't even call Anna, to see if her cold was better. Anna might have understood — maybe — but Zoe felt embarrassed to tell her. Anna would wonder why Zoe hadn't said anything to stop Lisa.

Even Ella probably wouldn't understand how Zoe felt. After all, everyone was always telling Ella what a smart, smart dog she was.

Chapter Nine

THE EID LANTERNS

The next day, Anna was still sick, and school wasn't any easier for Zoe than the day before.

Even though she often thought of how awful Lisa had been, even though Anna wasn't there, Zoe had thought the day would be fun, because she knew the class would be sampling foods from the Eid feast that Muslims enjoyed at the end of Ramadan, when they no longer had to fast.

Zoe loved food — especially trying new kinds. And for lunch that day there had been plenty of new dishes to try. There was lamb stuffed with rice, nuts, dates, and apricots. There was pita bread and yogurt, and chickpea salad, and there were lots of vegetables, like eggplant, and a big salad with olives. For dessert there were cookies with nuts and dates. Zoe was in heaven!

But then lunch ended.

Mrs. Green handed out construction paper, glue and scissors, and Zoe smelled trouble. She always found art difficult, because her fingers got stiff — especially when she grew nervous — and wouldn't move the way she wanted them to. She loved to tell stories, and write and hear stories or poems. She loved working on computers. She loved learning about maps and people and places. Math wasn't easy for her, but she liked doing puzzles. And music was her most favorite part of school!

But art was different. No matter how hard she worked, her projects in art class never turned out right.

⟡⟡⟡

Zoe glared down at the crooked shapes of gray and purple and yellow construction paper she had cut out. They were lying all over her desk, and her fingers were sticky with glue. The glue was drying all over her hands now, and that made her feel even more clumsy.

The project had seemed so simple! Mrs. Green, Yasmine and Samir had told them that Muslims used special lanterns called *fanoos* to decorate and light up their houses during the Eid celebration. Now they were making their own lanterns to decorate the classroom. Zoe was sure she was the only one not having fun doing it.

Mrs. Green had drawn lanterns on cardboard, one for each of them. And now they were pasting colored construction paper onto the drawings, so that the lanterns seemed to be made of colored glass. Everyone else's lantern looked so neat and pretty, Zoe thought sadly. Hers was a mess! She was so far behind the rest of the class, too! A lot of the children were already finished, and Mrs. Green was putting their lanterns up on the walls.

Zoe didn't want her lantern put up anywhere, for everybody else to see. They would all hate it. *She* hated it! She hated having hands that put crafts together all wrong. She hated needing her wheelchair. At that moment, she even hated needing Ella!

Zoe looked at the mess on her desk and wished she were doing something else. She wished Mrs. Green would stop putting up all those tidy lanterns and make them go over the math sheets handed out for homework the day before. She wanted to be doing *anything* but this!

"Mrs. Green, I think Zoe needs help. I don't think she can do this by herself."

Zoe looked up, stunned. She saw Lisa staring down at her sticky mess, and felt her face get hot. A lump rose in her throat, and the sick feeling in her stomach was back. Why did Lisa have to see how badly Zoe was doing? Why did it have to be *Lisa* standing over her now? Lisa already thought Zoe wasn't smart and couldn't do anything. Now it would be even worse!

She remembered playing dreidel with Lisa, and Lisa cheating, and Lisa laughing at her in class. This was more than she could take!

She turned toward Lisa, and her anger and frustration burst out.

"You think I can't do anything by myself! You think I'm not smart, just because I sit in a wheelchair and I need a dog to help me. You don't want to be my friend. You only want to *pretend* I can't do things, so you can make fun of me, and point at me, and laugh at me! I don't want anyone's help. I hate art anyway!"

Zoe wished she had quick arms and legs like everyone else, so that she could stomp out of the classroom and slam the door. But being upset made her body even stiffer than usual, and it took a very, very long time for her to roll her wheelchair to the door. And the door was closed, so then she had to wait for Ella to pull the handle down with her paws. Although Ella was good at this, it seemed to Zoe that it all happened way too slowly.

Everyone was staring at her. She didn't have to turn around to know that. She could feel everyone looking at her.

She hated how people stared. People were always staring at her. Because she was in a wheelchair. Because she dropped things. Because her dog had to help her. Because her body moved so slowly. Because they wanted to see how she managed in her wheelchair. Because, because, because!

✦✦✦

Outside in the hall, with Ella's head on her lap, Zoe cried for a minute, and then she began to feel better. But she had never lost her temper in class before. How would she face all the kids again? How could she ever go back? Maybe they didn't *want* her to go back. Mrs. Green hadn't even tried to stop her from leaving.

She started to cry again. Ella whimpered, and put a paw on Zoe's knee.

Chapter Ten

SAMIR AND ADAM

"Hi Zoe."

Zoe was so surprised to hear Samir's voice that she would have fallen over if she hadn't been belted into her seat.

She didn't know what to say.

"Hi Samir," came out of her mouth in a whisper.

For a minute, neither of them said anything. Then Samir surprised Zoe again.

"Mrs. Green was going to come out, but I asked her if I could come instead," he said shyly. "Because I know a little about how you feel."

It was Zoe's turn to stare.

How could he understand her? Samir was very good at art, and he wasn't in a wheelchair.

He didn't let her wonder for long. He began to explain what he meant.

"I didn't want to talk about Adam the other day, but I guess I can now. We're not friends anymore."

"Why?"

"Remember how the big festival of Eid comes at the end of the Ramadan fast? The fasting during Ramadan is really hard. It's not just that I'm not allowed to eat or drink until sunset every day, for a whole month. It's also hard because lots of people who aren't Muslim don't understand why I can't eat."

Zoe was puzzled. "Why do they care? Why is it any of their business?"

"That's what I want to tell you," Samir said. "Ramadan isn't always at exactly the same time every year. The dates change, just like they do for Easter or Thanksgiving. So sometimes Adam's birthday is during Ramadan, and sometimes it's not. Last year, Ramadan didn't start until after Adam's birthday, so I went to his party and I had hamburgers and cake and ice cream like everyone else. But this year his party was *during* Ramadan, and it was in the afternoon — before sunset — so I couldn't go."

"That makes sense," Zoe said. "Why would you go to a party where everybody has lots of food and you get nothing?"

"Adam thinks I could have broken my fast if I wanted to. So he says I'm not really his friend. But the fast is part of being Muslim. We fast during Ramadan because the Prophet Mohammed fasted before he wrote the Koran, and that's our holy book. It was written thousands of years ago, but it's really, really important, and the fast helps us honor the time when it was written. I *can't* break the fast, even if I want to. Fasting is supposed to help me learn discipline, to strengthen my faith and help me follow it even when it would be easier to go to a party and eat until I'm stuffed!"

Zoe saw that Samir was getting upset. "You don't have to talk about this anymore. I understand," she said.

"No, I *want* to talk about it. I've got to tell *someone* who understands! I'm frustrated because I shouldn't have had to worry about this during our holy month. Ramadan is a time for me to pray, be with my family, and give to the poor — not worry about someone who gets mad at me just because of something I have to do!"

"Did you try to explain things to Adam?" Zoe asked.

"Yeah. He didn't want to listen. He told me I was making stupid excuses, and he called me a loser. Now other kids are saying they won't invite me to their birthday parties, because I wouldn't go."

"That's not fair!" Zoe burst out, so fiercely that she

startled Ella. "It's horrible for him to call you a loser! I think *he's* the loser! Next year, *nobody* should go to his birthday party! "

Samir's shoulders sagged. "Don't say that," he said quietly. "He just doesn't get it, that's all."

Zoe wished instantly that she hadn't spoken that way. Here Samir was, trying to help her, and she had opened her big mouth instead of listening.

"Sorry, Samir. It's just that Anna and I are best friends, and I would never be rude to her the way Adam was to you. I like it that Anna and I are different."

"Anna's lucky." Samir paused, and then seemed to think of something else. "During Ramadan, I have to try extra hard not to get angry. I have to be patient with people who don't understand me, and why my life is different. I have to try my hardest to forgive them when they hurt my feelings. That's not easy, especially now," he said. "It's my big challenge! When I get upset, it helps to remember all the people who do understand me. And — well, that's why I said I sort of understand how you feel."

❦❦❦

Zoe and Samir sat together quietly for a minute. Then Mrs. Green came out and asked Zoe if she was okay, and said they should go back into class. So Zoe and Samir went back together, and he helped her finish her *fanoo*. It wasn't perfect, but it looked pretty good. And while they worked on it, Zoe kept thinking about what Samir had said.

He had been telling her that people in wheelchairs weren't the only ones who felt misunderstood or frustrated or left out. Other people had things they couldn't do, or weren't allowed to do. Sometimes they too were teased about being different. Sometimes other people were rude about what they couldn't do, and sometimes people said mean things and told lies. Sometimes people thought they knew the truth about someone, but they didn't really know at all.

So even though Samir's situation was different from Zoe's, he could imagine how she felt when people didn't understand her. He could guess how hurt she was when people thought that if she had to use a wheelchair, she must not be very smart.

Samir knew how unfair it was that some people noticed what made Zoe different, without noticing that in many, many ways she was just like everyone else!

Chapter Eleven
THE BIRTHDAY PARTY

"I have one rule," Nalini announced. "You can all order anything you want. My treat!"

They were trying a new restaurant in the shopping mall. They were all seated at a long table, with Zoe in her wheelchair at one end. Ella was under the table as usual, hoping somebody would drop something yummy.

"But Nalini," Zoe's dad protested, "it's *your* birthday! Shouldn't we be taking *you* out for dinner?"

Nalini looked around the table as she answered, smiling at Ruby, at Zoe and Simon and their parents, at Simon's friend William, and at Anna and her mother.

"My birthday present is to have my family and friends around me, enjoying themselves. When I came to this country, I was very poor and I knew almost no one. I had been here for just a week when my birthday came around, and I spent it all alone. So I promised myself that I would make lots of good friends and I would celebrate with them every time I had a chance, and make sure everyone had a fantastic time. That means all of you, so…cheers!"

Nalini raised her glass, and everyone followed. "Now, as I said, all of you order whatever you want, and enjoy the party. Tonight, it's my job to spoil *you* rotten. Understood?"

✦✦✦

The restaurant was busy, and they waited a long time before the waitress came. Zoe had pretty much decided on spaghetti and meatballs, but then Simon spoke up.

"Hey, Will, look at this cool cheeseburger! With fries *and* onion rings! That's what I want!"

For a minute, Zoe was tempted to change her mind. But maybe she could sneak some fries off Simon's plate.

"All I know is, *I'm* saving room for dessert," William said, smiling from ear to ear. "Listen to this: 'Two scoops of chocolate ice cream with marshmallow sauce, with butterscotch chips and pecans on top.' Wow!"

Zoe's mother and Mrs. Myers rolled their eyes, but Nalini just laughed.

That was when the waitress came. She leaned in past Zoe and took everyone else's order. Then she asked the others, "And is this little girl eating too?"

"I'll have the spaghetti and meatballs, and an iced tea, please and thank you," Zoe said firmly, so the woman would know she could speak for herself.

"The spaghetti might be hard for her to eat," the waitress said doubtfully, still ignoring Zoe and talking to her parents instead. Zoe's stomach dropped, and her throat was suddenly dry. She felt everyone watching her to see what she would do, what she would say. But she knew they were all on her side. She looked at Anna for strength, took a deep breath, and said:

"It's my dinner, so you can talk to me about it. I told you I wanted spaghetti and meatballs, and I still want spaghetti and meatballs. I'll be fine."

"I'll have the chef cut up her spaghetti," the waitress said, again to Zoe's parents.

And she was gone.

☜☜☜

It happened again, too.

When Zoe asked the waitress for a second iced tea that evening, she also asked for a straw.

"Oh sure, I'll bring her one," the woman said. "But does she need me to put the drink in a cup instead of a glass?" Once more, she spoke directly to Zoe's parents.

Zoe didn't give anyone a chance to answer for her. "No, thank you," she said quickly. "A glass is *just fine.*"

She didn't want to cry. She didn't want to ruin Nalini's birthday. But it was hard to swallow past the lump growing in her throat.

As for the others, they were all furious.

"I'm never coming to this restaurant again," Nalini fumed. "And when that waitress comes back, I'm going to give her a piece of my mind for the way she's treating you, Zoe!"

"No, you're not," Zoe answered. "I am. In fact, I'm going to put it in writing."

Zoe's mother gave her a page from the notepad she kept in her purse.

Ruby gave her a pen.

Zoe wrote the note:

Hi,

You are hurting my feelings when you talk to other people about what I order, and what you think I need. If I needed my spaghetti to be cut up, I would have asked for that. If I needed to drink from a cup and not a glass, I would have told you that. I am a real person, just as my family and my friends are.

Zoe

When they left the restaurant, Zoe's note stayed behind, propped up against her empty glass, where the waitress was sure to find it.

Chapter Twelve
THE MEANING OF ZOE

Around bedtime that night, Zoe was lying in bed with Ella sitting on the rug beside her. Zoe could just reach far enough to stroke her furry friend's head. She lay quietly, petting Ella and scratching her gently behind the ears.

"It's not fair, Ella! Why does everything have to be so hard?" She could feel that lump in her throat again. Ella sensed her unhappiness. She rested her chin on the bed, and gazed at Zoe with those big brown eyes.

"What's the matter, Zoe?"

Zoe turned her head and saw that her mother had come in. She wasn't sure her mother could help her with what she was feeling. But then, she had not expected Samir to understand her frustration when she lost her temper in art class. He *had* understood, though. He had helped her.

So Zoe told her mother everything. She told her about Lisa and the game of dreidel. She told her about feeling that she couldn't do anything right while she was working on her paper lantern, about shouting at Lisa in class, and about how Lisa had been even meaner to her since that day. She told her about feeling left out because she never got a real adventure. People worried about her too much, as if they were afraid she would break.

They worried too much, or they ignored Zoe because they saw her wheelchair and wouldn't believe that she could think or speak for herself — like that waitress. She had acted as if Zoe wasn't there, as if she had no voice and no brain! She had made Zoe feel so small!

"When Anna dances or skates, she tells me how free that makes her feel, as if she could fly," Zoe explained, the tears coming back. "When am I ever going to feel like that, stuck in my wheelchair? My stupid, stupid wheelchair!"

Her mother thought for a moment. "Well," she said, "don't you remember when you saw those kittens being born on Aunt Jessica's farm? Wasn't that exciting?"

"Of course it was, Mom. And I learned a lot, but I *watched* that happen. I want to do things, *make* things happen, you know?"

"Don't forget what a big help you were when Ella got sprayed by the skunk. You were the one who thought of finding Nalini, and you took charge and calmed Ella down when she was a very upset dog. Wasn't that kind of an adventure?"

"Mom, Ella stank after that! It wasn't any fun for anybody. Nobody enjoyed it! How can *that* be an adventure?"

Zoe punched her pillow hard, so hard that she surprised herself with the power of her own fist. She rested her head against the pillow and sighed deeply — an exasperated, frustrated sigh. "You just don't understand," she complained. Ella whimpered a little. She didn't like to see Zoe upset.

Zoe reached over and scratched Ella under her chin, and began to feel better.

"Sorry," she said quietly after a moment.

"No, it's all right," her mom said gently. "You can punch your pillow again, if you want. It might help."

So she understood. And she wasn't angry. She didn't even look surprised at anything Zoe had said. She just let her finish, and then she asked, "Do you know why we chose to give you the name 'Zoe'?"

Zoe shook her head.

"*Zoe* is Greek for 'life,'" her mother explained.

"When you were born, I wanted a baby so very much.

I couldn't wait to take care of you and watch you grow! From the first time I held you, you seemed so excited to be alive. You wiggled and wiggled and snuggled close to me. You even smiled at me before you fell asleep that first time. You knew that you were safe, and that you had gotten to where you needed to be.

"We knew you would live a life that was important. So we gave you a name that means 'life' because we wanted your name to remind you that life is a gift. There are happy parts and sad parts. There are exciting parts and boring parts. There are funny parts and scary parts, easy parts and hard parts. We all wish there weren't sad or scary or boring or hard parts. But those are the parts that teach us how to have patience and courage. If we never went through anything scary or hard, we wouldn't have any idea how to help someone else who is scared and having a hard time. We wouldn't know how to be strong.

"When you were upset in art class and Samir came and talked to you, he knew how to help you feel better because he was having a hard time too. He might not have understood your feelings if he hadn't felt frustrated and alone himself.

"Sometimes, when we're busy living from day to day and getting through the parts of life we'd rather do without, it hardly feels like an adventure. But adventures don't happen when we expect them, when we're waiting for them. We have to let them sneak up on us. They don't tell us they're coming! Just because you need help sometimes, that doesn't mean you won't have adventures. It just means that other people will be lucky enough to have them with you, so you can all enjoy your adventures together! Does that help you feel a little better?"

"A little," Zoe admitted. "That waitress tonight is still bugging me, though. I don't think she learned anything. All those times I spoke up didn't make any difference. She still treated me like a baby. She might not read my note when she finds it. And even if she does, she probably won't believe I really wrote it. She'll think Simon or Ruby or William pretended to be me. She doesn't think I'm smart, remember? It's no use. The next time she serves somebody in a wheelchair, she'll just act the same way again."

"It's true that we don't know for sure if that waitress will ever change," Zoe's mother said gently. "Some people have no idea how to behave in a situation they're not used to, like talking to someone in a wheelchair. Sometimes they want to learn, and sometimes they don't. When they don't, all you can do is speak up for yourself and hope that some day they start understanding. People's attitudes are changing. They're getting better. It's just that change happens slowly…sometimes one person at a time. But don't focus on people like her. Have fun with all the people who *do* treat you like the smart girl you are, the people who love you and make you happy. Live the very best life you can. Needing help with some things, even being frightened sometimes, doesn't mean that you are helpless or that you'll never do anything really exciting."

She kissed Zoe on the cheek.

"I want you to remember two things for me. Remember what you're learning at school right now. People have different traditions and celebrate their beliefs in different ways, but no matter what, everyone is special. And remember that it doesn't matter that your disability makes you move a little more slowly, or that you look different because you have a wheelchair. People have lots of ways to move around and get things done. Some use cars, some use bicycles, some use horses, some use canes or walkers...."

Zoe laughed. "Some use skateboards!" Simon wanted to go *everywhere* on his skateboard.

"That's right! There are lots of ways to get around, and lots of ways to have adventures. That's part of what makes the world exciting. Can you imagine how boring it would be if we were all exactly the same, and we all did everything the same way? Just look at my family! Aren't we all different?"

Zoe laughed again, thinking of her tall, thin Aunt Beth, the dancer, with her black clothes and funky jewelry, and her round little Aunt Jessica, who lived on a farm, loved to cook, and smelled of rosemary and mint. She always called Zoe food names, like "pumpkin" and "lambchop." And then there was her mother, the bookworm, who never did anything without reading about it first. The three of them were as different as could be.

"Having a disability makes some things harder," her mother admitted. "But your life has lots of good parts, too! You have me and your father, and Simon and William. You have Mrs. Green. You have Anna and her mom, and Samir, and Nalini and Ruby. You have Grandma, too, and all your aunts and uncles and cousins. And Grandpa loved you very much. We all think you're wonderful!"

"I have Ella, too. Don't forget Ella!" Zoe reminded her mother. "She's such a good dog. She's my friend too. I don't like needing help, but I *love* Ella."

Ella looked up from her bed happily when she heard her name.

"I know you do," Zoe's mother said. "We all do." She gave Zoe a hug.

"Good night. Sleep tight," she said, as she turned off the bedroom light and quietly closed the door.

"Zoe means life," Zoe murmured to herself. "And life is a gift, even if it has some hard parts. I'll remember that. Good night, Ella."

Whump, whump, whump, went the tail on the floor.

Chapter Thirteen
DIVALI LIGHTS

The next week, the class talked about Divali, the Hindu Festival of Lights. Nalini came to class to tell them about some Divali traditions, and to show photos of her trip to India with Ruby. Last year, they had celebrated Divali there.

The class sat in a circle, looking at the pictures and feeling stuffed; they had just had a Divali feast, thanks to Nalini. There was vegetable curry with mango chutney, samosas, Indian bread called *puri*, rice pudding, fruit cream…so much food! Ever since Zoe had become friends with Ruby and had started trying Nalini's food, she had loved the flavors and spices.

If it hadn't been for the colorful photos, Zoe might have fallen asleep because she was so full.

"Wow! There are a lot of little lights in this one. What does it mean?" Heather asked, as the next photo being passed around the circle reached her.

"Those are *diva* lamps," Nalini explained. "We light them as part of the Divali tradition. Since we believe that light is a gift and a sign of good, we do this to honor beauty and knowledge, and to drive away hatred, anger, and selfishness. Divali is the Hindu New Year. It's a time to celebrate light, hope, prosperity, and strength spent on helping people. Our festival is five days long, and there is always plenty of food, sweets, and presents."

"Let's not talk about food right now," Zoe groaned.

Ruby giggled.

"During Divali, we also go to our temple to receive blessings and wish everyone a happy new year!" Nalini continued. "We visit with family and friends..."

"Hey, look at *this* picture! Look at Ruby, the dancing cleaning lady!" Samir laughed, holding up a picture. It showed Ruby dancing with a mop, smiling at the camera. She snatched the picture away from Samir good-naturedly while her grandmother went on.

"To prepare for Divali, we clean our homes very carefully, because we believe that clean homes are blessed for the coming year," Nalini told them. "As you can see, Ruby took her job very seriously. We cleaned my brother's house, and then we decorated inside and outside with diva lamps. We put them in clay pots and sat them close to our doors and windows, and in the garden. We also had lots of flowers, and at the entrance we placed intricate designs made with grains of colored rice."

"You should have seen India during Divali," Ruby remembered. "It was beautiful! The streets in Delhi were full of lights. Every building was decorated with lights, and we lit firecrackers! It was so much fun...."

"Who's with you in this picture, Nalini?" Zoe asked, holding up a photo of Nalini standing beside a tall, thin man. They looked so happy, their arms tightly around each other.

Nalini's eyes were suddenly wet, and she dabbed them quickly with a tissue before she spoke. "That's my younger brother, Vikram," she said. "He lives in India, and I miss him very much. All my other brothers and sisters were older than me, and they've already passed away."

In another moment, though, Nalini was back to her old self. "The last day of Divali is an important day for brothers and sisters," she continued. "Sisters invite their brothers over for dinner, and brothers bring gifts for their sisters, like jewelry or a new sari, which is a traditional Hindu dress, like the one I'm wearing today."

Everyone had noticed Nalini's long dress, made of

lovely green material that swept around her and reached to her ankles. "Vikram gave me this sari," she said proudly. "We dress in bright new clothes to celebrate Divali. Girls and women use a colored dye called henna to create beautiful designs on their skin."

"Show them your paintings now," Ruby begged her grandmother.

As she walked around the circle and gathered up the photos, Nalini laughed warmly at her granddaughter's eagerness. "Ruby is proud of me because I'm an artist, and I paint a lot," she said. "I'm always getting ready for art shows, where people come to see my work and buy it. Every year, during our Festival of Lights, we send our family and friends Divali cards to wish them well, and I also sell these cards to companies. Today, I brought some cards with my paintings on them. I'm sending them around for you to see. Be very careful with them, just as you were with the photos! Make sure you put them back on this table when you're done, in a neat pile, please."

Zoe saw a wonderful painting coming toward her, going from hand to hand around the circle — a painting of a wide river with many small diva lamps floating on the water like bright, shining boats. There was so much light in the painting — light from the lamps, and light from their reflections in the water. In the painting, there were many people along the shore, watching the lamps dance on the river.

"This is so beautiful!" Zoe exclaimed, holding the print in her hand.

"Thank you," Nalini said. "You see, in India, during Divali, we also float diva lamps on the water as part of the celebration."

Nalini drew and painted so beautifully, it took Zoe's breath away.

There were lots of Nalini's other paintings to see, too — one of fireworks exploding in the sky, another of hands decorated with henna.

When she saw the decorated hands, Zoe beamed. This weekend, Nalini had promised to draw henna designs on Zoe's hands, for the first time ever. She was so excited!

"Nalini, can you bring henna to class?" Heather wanted to know. "I love these designs! Can you draw some on our skin?"

She read my mind, Zoe thought.

"Yeah, that would be so cool!" Angie exclaimed.

"I'd love to," Nalini said. "But I don't think it would be a good idea."

"Why not?"

"Henna designs are complicated. They're made with

paste from the henna plant. The leaves are ground up and dried to make the paste. Once the designs are drawn on your skin, the paste needs to stay there for about six hours. You would need to stay as still as you can for all that time. If you smudge the designs, they'll be ruined. But you can't stay still for that long while you're at school!"

"How does *anyone* stay still for that long?"

"Does henna wash off?"

"Is it always red, like in this picture?"

"Does it smell?"

"How long do the designs last?"

"Whoa! So many questions! One at a time, please! I can't answer you all at once! It *is* hard to stay still for that long. Most people secure the paste in place with bandages or plastic wrap, and go to bed for the night. In the morning, the paste is taken off and the designs remain. They usually fade and wash off in one to three weeks on thicker skin, like your hands, feet, and ankles. On thinner skin, like on your arms or your back, they only last about ten days."

"What color is —"

"I was just getting to that. Henna powder is green, and it has a strong smell, kind of like fresh hay. But once the paste is dry on your skin, it turns orangey-yellow, and then finally reddish-brown."

Lisa's voice interrupted Nalini. "Are we gonna do a Divali craft?"

"I think you'll be decorating the classroom with colored rice designs tomorrow, Lisa."

"Uh-oh," Lisa said quickly, in a low voice. "Zoe might throw another screaming fit!" She spoke quietly enough that Mrs. Green and Nalini didn't hear.

But Zoe did.

Her breath caught in her throat, and she felt suddenly cold. Zoe wanted to scream, but instead she bent down to Ella, who snuggled close as Zoe stroked her. Zoe didn't want anyone to see the hurt on her face. She gulped, taking deep breaths as she remembered her mother's words last week. *Sometimes people want to change, and sometimes they don't.* Well, Zoe knew Lisa didn't. And there was nothing she could do about it.

That made Zoe feel sad, but in a strange way she also felt free. It wasn't her job to fix Lisa's attitude. She had tried, and it hadn't worked. No, she would think of the good parts of her life. She would move on.

She straightened up, held her head high, and listened to the rest of Nalini's lesson.

"You have beautiful hands, Zoe."

Nalini's words hung in the air as Zoe stared at her own hands: the long fingers, and the way the light from Nalini's kitchen window shone on them. Zoe wouldn't call them beautiful. They let her down too often.

But she kept that to herself. To Nalini she said, "They're okay. The design you're drawing on them is great."

"But you don't think your hands are beautiful?"

"Well…there is so much my hands aren't good at, and sometimes that makes me sad."

Nalini looked at her for a long moment, in a way that let Zoe know she was about to say something important, something to remember.

"Your hands are part of the mystery of your life. You are very young, and right now you don't know everything your life will hold, or what these hands will do. But I promise you, you are already amazing."

ᛣᛣᛣ

And then it was Wednesday.

Watching Anna in class while she studied fractions, wrote a story in her journal, and worked on a puzzle, Zoe thought her friend looked even happier than usual. Many times during the day, she caught Anna looking at her and then looking away, and getting back to work with a smile on her face.

It seemed to Zoe that Anna was keeping an exciting secret.

✯✯✯

The next day marked Ella's anniversary. She had been Zoe's dog for two whole years!

There were doggy presents waiting for her after school: a brand new yellow collar and leash, a new ball with a squeaker inside, and a chew toy shaped like a bone, along with a fleecy green blanket. Zoe stroked her dog lovingly as she slipped the new collar over Ella's head. Her mother put the new chew toy near Ella's favorite spot in the kitchen, and spread the blanket where the dog slept beside Zoe's bed.

Zoe whispered in Ella's ear:

"These are for you, Ella. Happy anniversary! Thank you for being my wonderful friend. I love you!"

"Do you think Ella likes her gifts?" her mother asked.

"She thinks they're amazing!" Zoe told her.

"Then what will she think about *this*?" And right before Zoe's eyes, her closet door popped open, and all around her she heard, *"Surprise!!!!"*

Out of the closet came Simon and Ruby and Anna and Samir. Then Anna's mother came in from across the hall, holding a cake that had *Thank you, Ella, and welcome, Cinder!* written in pink icing across the top.

Zoe felt weak with delight when she saw that Anna had a beautiful puppy wiggling in her arms — the one she had dreamed would be hers.

"Come and hold Cinder, Zoe!" said Anna, beaming.

Together, everyone sang, "For these are jolly good doggies, that nobody can deny!"

After they had the cake, Ruby danced a graceful Divali dance that Nalini had taught her, wearing a beautiful, brightly colored sari that Nalini had given her. Her long hair was pinned up in a bun.

Zoe knew that Ruby had spent lots of time learning the dance. She watched her friend sway and turn to the music from one of Nalini's CDs. She enjoyed the dance, but she felt a little left out. *She* would never get to dance like that. It made her feel sad again. Oh, how she wished she could dance that way!

But then she remembered all of the things her mother had told her, and she began to feel better. After all, she was important too, and lots of people loved her. Soon she forgot about being sad. She was too busy laughing, watching Cinder chase Ella in circles.

That gave Anna an idea. Before Zoe knew it, Anna was spinning Zoe in circles in her wheelchair, and they were dancing together in their own way. They laughed and danced, and danced and laughed, with Cinder yipping happily and Ella looking *very* confused. Soon enough, everyone was laughing and dancing.

While they danced, it began to snow. Finally, winter was really here.

Chapter Fourteen
THE SECRET

He hadn't meant to overhear anything.

Simon walked through the newly fallen snow on his morning paper route. On a Sunday, and trudging through the first thick, lasting blanket of snow of the year, he should not have been worried. He should have been dreaming of hockey, not fussing about his kid sister. But he couldn't help it.

He had been standing outside Zoe's door at the beginning of the week, about to go in to pet Ella and say good night, the way he always did. But he had heard Zoe crying and Mom talking to her softly, and he had stayed outside the door.

Listening.

He had heard how frustrated Zoe was, and how much she wanted a real adventure. Wasn't that something a big brother should be able to find? He had been thinking about it for days. He had thought and thought, looked and looked for ideas.

He was still looking.

But he could hear their parents in his mind.

Watch Zoe's head!

Don't let her fall!

Be gentle with her!

Be careful!

There had to be a way to be careful and still have *real* fun....

✗✗✗

"Good morning, Simon."

Nalini's voice reached him, floating on the air, as he passed the park.

She's up early, he thought, scanning the park. There she was, wearing her green winter coat and grinning from ear to ear as she pulled a toboggan up the hill. Ruby was with her grandmother, her cheeks rosy and her ponytail swinging.

Simon walked quickly toward them, excitement swirling in his head.

A toboggan.

He felt the smile in his toes.

"Nalini, I have an idea, and I need your help."

✦✦✦

As Simon shook Zoe gently, early the next Sunday morning, his heart beat fast.

"Come on, Zoe, up you get!" he coaxed urgently, in a whisper.

Zoe groaned. "Simon, what are you…talking… about?"

"I'm talking about a surprise."

"Simon, it's six o'clock in the…."

"I know what time it is, but it's worth it," he said, slowly peeling back the warm covers as Zoe half-tried to tug them up again.

But even through the fog of sleep, the word "surprise" had reached her.

In a moment she was sitting on the edge of the bed, rubbing her eyes as Ella licked her face. "What's going on?"

"Get dressed fast and you'll find out."

Simon rummaged through Zoe's closet until he found a cozy outfit.

"Here, put these on, quick. We need to get out of here before Mom and Dad wake up."

"Those are *sweat pants*, Simon," Zoe objected. "I don't wear those except for when I'm exercising. You know that!"

Simon couldn't help rolling his eyes. "Shhhh! Keep your voice down. I'm trying to find warm clothes that are easy for you to put on, and fast. Come on, Ella, move over! We have to get going. Do you want to have a real blast, Zoe, or not?"

A smile spread across Zoe's face. "Mom and Dad don't know what we're doing?"

"No, and let's keep it that way. Get dressed and meet me at the front door."

That got Zoe moving!

�✚✚

Zoe tried to get hints out of Simon all the way to Nalini's house, but it didn't work. When Nalini came out carrying a pair of snow pants that Zoe recognized as Ruby's, she was even more excited — and astonished. Pushing Zoe's wheelchair up the planks of wood that she used as a wheelchair ramp, Nalini said, "You're going to have quite a morning, my dear! Let's get started!"

"I have my own snow pants, but Simon didn't tell me to bring them," Zoe explained, as Nalini helped her put Ruby's pants on over her clothes, in her sewing room.

"He had a good reason. Soon you'll understand," Nalini told her, with a wink and a huge grin.

Zoe looked around the sewing room, at all the brightly colored material Nalini used to make saris. So much color...red, yellow, blue, green, even gold. It reminded Zoe of a jungle full of gorgeous parrots.

"It's all so beautiful, Nalini!" she breathed. "I can't wait to see the saris you make. You're so good with your hands. You sew, you paint, you draw henna designs. I just wish my hands could...."

Nalini looked stern. "It's time you learned to like your own hands, Zoe. No more of this! I want to show you something. Come with me."

Zoe and Ella followed her through the house to the back. Nalini opened the door to her art studio, where she kept all her drawings and paintings. Ruby and Zoe were hardly ever allowed in there.

"How come...?"

"Just a minute. You'll see. But Ella will need to stay here. I'm sorry, Ella."

They went inside, and Zoe looked around. There were paintings and drawings along all the walls, and lots of easels. Some of Nalini's work on the easels looked finished, or almost there. Other pieces were half done, and still others were barely started.

Zoe stared at a beautiful framed painting on the wall, of trees in a forest, with the sun shining through their leaves. There was a drawing of Ruby laughing, and a painting of a lake, and geese flying over it.

Zoe thought, *It's so real, I want to jump in that lake.*

"It's this one I want you to see," Nalini said, interrupting her thoughts. The minute Zoe saw the painting on the other side of the room, she remembered looking at the copy of it in class. It was the painting of the river in India, with diva lamps floating in it.

"I remember this one. You brought the copy of it to class. I love it!" Zoe told her.

"I wanted to show it to you again, because I want to tell you that when we put the lamps in the river, we never know *exactly* where they'll be carried as the water flows, but the light from our lamps makes the river beautiful, wherever they go. It's the same with your hands, Zoe. They're beautiful. They aren't perfect, but nothing is. They are part of you, and one day you will see that they make many things possible, just as they are. "

As she spoke, Nalini walked to a table, opened a drawer, and handed Zoe a copy of the same painting, the size of a postcard.

"I'm giving you this so you can keep it with you. I hope it always reminds you of what I've said."

"Thank you," Zoe said, a lump in her throat.

Nalini clapped her hands. "Enough seriousness!" she declared. "We've left Ella waiting, and Simon, too. Let's get this show on the road!"

Chapter Fifteen

ZOE'S AMAZING ADVENTURE

The world was whizzing by.

Zoe was laughing so hard that she was nearly crying with joy, watching snow and trees flash past in a blur as she zoomed down the hill on the toboggan.

"Wheeeee!"

Snow was flying in all directions, and the wind frosted her face. She could feel the speed everywhere: under her, as they skimmed down the hill; in her stomach, as it dropped as if she was on an elevator, each time they hit a bump; in her chest, as her heart thumped with the thrill of it all.

So *this* is what tobogganing felt like!

Nalini sat behind Zoe, with her arms around her, and Simon was behind Nalini. Ruby sat on the very back of the toboggan. They were all laughing and whooping helplessly. Ella dashed after the toboggan, galumphing through the snow and barking for joy.

Now, *this* was adventure!

But there was one small problem.

The first time they reached the bottom of the hill, worry began to creep into Zoe's mind. How would they get her to the top again? She really, *really* didn't want to be lifted — but how else…?

Then Nalini emerged from behind a tree with a push-broom that she attached to the back of the toboggan, as a sort of handle. There was a clip on the toboggan rope, and Nalini attached it to Ella's harness, so that she could help too. With Nalini pushing, Simon, Ruby and Ella pulling, and Zoe hanging on for dear life, they soon made their way back up the hill.

"Many hands make light work!" called out Nalini as they crested the hill.

↟↟↟

"We should go home now, Zoe," Nalini said, after the fifth trip down the hill. "I don't want you to get too tired."

"I'm not tired, I *promise*. One more ride Nalini, *please!* Just one more…"

111

✖✖✖

After six trips down the hill, Zoe finally agreed it was time to go home. It was so cold that her nose was running, her cheeks had gone numb, her teeth hurt and the snow was soaking through her pants.

But she had had the most *awesome* time!

"Thank you, everyone, for everything," she exclaimed. "I'll remember this forever!"

"Well," said Ruby, "at least till next Sunday. Because we're coming back again, you know."

"Again!" Zoe didn't know whether to laugh or cry. "I — oh, look at Ella!" Ella had gone for one last run down the hill, and she'd run so fast that she'd landed head over heels in the snow!

✖✖✖

On the way home, Zoe learned how hard Simon, Nalini, and Ruby had worked to make this adventure happen. They had done all the planning, and they had kept everything secret so Mom and Dad wouldn't find out and stop them to protect Zoe.

Simon had spoken to the woman in charge of his Sunday morning paper route, and she had let him switch to Saturday mornings, so he'd be free on Sundays for their secret toboggan rides.

Nalini had agreed to help, even letting Zoe wear Ruby's old snow pants, and promising to take them home and dry them in time for next week. After all, if Mom and Dad saw that Zoe's own snow pants were soaking wet, they would know *something* was going on!

↟↟↟

Zoe didn't know that Lisa had been watching them. Lisa lived beside the park, and her bedroom overlooked the toboggan hill. From her window, she could see and hear the games and cheering of the kids who played there.

On that first Sunday, all the laughter of the toboggan rides drifted through her windows and woke Lisa up. It was unusual for people to toboggan so early. She pulled on her robe, went to the window and peered out.

She saw Simon, Nalini, Ruby...and Zoe!

Zoe in a toboggan, shrieking with laughter, sliding down the hill. Ella was there too, running behind the toboggan. But where was Zoe's wheelchair?

Lisa had never seen Zoe without her wheelchair. She looked like a different person. Or — no — she didn't look *different* at all.

✦✦✦

All that week, when Simon needed anything from Zoe, he didn't have to ask twice. And the next Sunday, he didn't even have to wake her up. When he came to her room, she was already dressed and moving from her bed to her wheelchair.

This time, Anna and William came for the toboggan rides too, along with Nalini and Ruby, and Ella, of course. They had a wonderful time rocketing down the hill in the crisp air of early morning. And getting back up the hill was even easier, with more people to help. They all hoped and hoped the snow wouldn't melt, when they agreed to meet again the following weekend.

Once more, Lisa was standing at her window, seeing everything.

Chapter Sixteen

CATS AND BIRDS

"Everybody's coming to my house for hot chocolate and sweets after lunch today!" Nalini announced, after the toboggan rides the following week.

"Can't we come *now*?" William pleaded. He and Simon were always thinking about food.

"No, you're not allowed sweets before breakfast! But we'll have such a good time this afternoon, I promise. See you all after lunch!"

✦✦✦

So it was that Zoe found herself, Simon and their friends all sitting in Nalini's kitchen, sipping hot chocolate at the big kitchen table. Ella lay beside the table, gnawing on her new chew toy.

Zoe took a deep breath.

"Thank you, Nalini, for helping Simon and Ruby plan these toboggan rides. They're the best! We're having so much fun!"

"You're welcome, Zoe. I've been riding my toboggan for years, and keeping all the fun to myself. But now I know how much I've been missing all this time. It's even better with all of you!"

"Wait a minute," Simon piped up. "You've been tobogganing by yourself? But why...?"

"Yeah," William chorused. "You're supposed to be a grandmother."

"*William!*" Ruby exclaimed, looking shocked. "My grandmother is *cool!*"

Nalini laughed, a great, cheery sound. Zoe couldn't help thinking that Nalini was full of things no one expected, like that huge, bubbling sound coming out of such a small lady. Small, but strong in so many ways, Zoe knew.

"It's okay, William," Nalini reassured him, with her big smile. "I'm full of surprises! That keeps me young. That's why I started tobogganing. Where I come from in India, there is no snow. There's either sun or rain. So when I came to this country, I couldn't wait for it to snow so I could see it with my own eyes. And I loved it. So white and soft, and every flake so beautiful. It was a new beginning for me — just like living here was a new beginning. All of you know," Nalini said — and she winked at Zoe — "that tobogganing is such an *adventure!* I toboggan as much as I can. It's like magic! It makes me excited and happy."

"You're always happy, Nalini," Simon pointed out.

"Oh, not always. But I try."

Nalini paused and sipped her hot chocolate. There was a faraway look in her eye, as though she was remembering something from a long time ago. Then she got up from her chair and brought over a box with the name of a bakery on top. "Sweet Dreams," it said.

She opened the box, and the children craned their necks to see inside.

"This is a traditional Greek sweet called baklava. It has layers and layers of pastry sprinkled with nuts and honey," she explained.

"But you're not Greek," Zoe blurted.

"No, I'm not Greek, but the first friends I made when I came here were Greek. They owned a bakery and they lived right above it. They invited me in for wonderful meals and desserts. Their grandchildren taught me how to toboggan. So tobogganing always makes me think of them.

"Here, everyone, try some. But watch out, they're dribbly."

★★★

While everyone was busy eating, Mustang walked into the kitchen with a small gray and white cat that Zoe didn't recognize. Mustang gave Ella the usual wary look and made a large circle around her, keeping as far away from her as he could. The other cat followed Mustang nervously, arching its back and hissing at the sight of the dog. Ella yawned and rolled over.

Everyone around the table laughed at the show.

"Nalini, you didn't tell me you got another cat!" Zoe cried.

Nalini stopped laughing. "Well...I didn't, exactly. That's Laya, the Carters' cat. I'm looking after her for a while. The Carters live in that condo at the end of the block, and they need a hand right now."

"You're looking after *Lisa's* cat?" Zoe exclaimed. "Lisa Carter from my class? Lisa who cheated at dreidel and laughed at me and stole my chocolate and made that stupid comment about me during your Divali lesson? How could you, Nalini? I can't *stand* her! Whose side are you on, anyway?"

Nalini stared at Zoe. The others were watching her too. Zoe began to squirm. "It's just that…she really hurt my feelings." Zoe was suddenly quiet, surprised at her own anger.

"I don't like what Lisa did, either," Nalini said, gently squeezing Zoe's hand. "But I'm not taking care of Laya just for Lisa. It's a favor for her family. The Carters are good neighbors, no matter what mistakes Lisa made. They help me out a lot, and I need to return the favor. That's what good neighbors do: help each other. I won't make Lisa a better person by holding a grudge. I'll only make myself feel awful and spiteful. Let's learn from what Lisa did. Let's learn what *not* to do. Okay?"

She gave Zoe a hug. "Don't be mad at me, please."

"I'm not mad at you. I just haven't forgiven *her*."

"I know."

"I guess I still have a lot to learn," Zoe confided.

"Don't we all? But Zoe, listen. Lisa's grandmother is getting older, and she has to move out of the house she loves, and move in with the Carters, so they can help her take care of herself. Grandma Carter really, really wants to bring her two parakeets, Flora and Beau. But you know how cats and birds don't always get along, so…."

"So you're taking care of Laya, so the birds will be safe."

"Exactly."

Zoe was silent for a while, thinking of Jade, the parakeet she and Simon had had when she was small. Zoe had been so sad when Jade died, just a while before Ella came along.

You have such a way with that bird, Zoe, her father always used to say.

"Does that help you understand why I offered to help?" Nalini's question brought Zoe back to the present.

A little, Zoe thought to herself. *I have to think about it, but I'll get there.*

Out loud, though, she said, "Nalini, you're amazing. You're ready for just about anything, aren't you?"

"Most of the time, Zoe. Most of the time."

Chapter Seventeen

THE ACCIDENT

They had just arrived at the park. Today would be even better, because Anna had brought Cinder along.

And then it happened, in the blink of an eye.

One minute Nalini was skimming down the hill, taking the first toboggan run of the day by herself. Watching Nalini, Cinder couldn't stay still. She surged forward against Anna's grip on her leash, eager to follow the fun.

"I can't hold her *back!*" Anna shrieked. "Cinder! Cinder! *No!*"

The next minute, Cinder was careering down the hill, chasing Nalini's toboggan, running directly in its path!

They all gasped, and Anna shrieked, "My *puppy!* Nalini! Stop! *Please stop!!* Cinder's gonna get hurt!"

Nalini swerved the toboggan, wrenching it sideways and out of Cinder's way.

And the toboggan tipped over. Nalini tumbled off, catching her foot in the toboggan as she fell.

Everyone ran to her. Everyone except Zoe, who was still sitting in her wheelchair at the top of the hill. Ella and Cinder got there first, and washed Nalini's face with their tongues.

"Are you all right?" asked Simon.

"Grandma, did you hurt yourself?" Ruby asked anxiously.

"Can you stand up?" asked William.

"I'm fine, I'm fine!" Nalini insisted, waving them away. "My ankle just hurts a bit. See? I can stand."

But there was pain on her face. She could not stand up. Trying made her wince.

Anna was choked with tears, hugging her rescued puppy close. "I'm so *sorry*, Nalini! I should *never* have brought Cinder with me today!"

"This is no one's fault," Nalini objected. "Sometimes these things just happen, that's all. Don't worry."

Simon trudged back up the hill to Zoe, looking serious. "I'm sorry, Zoe, but I have to go and get Dad to help," he said.

"Rubbish!" Nalini objected loudly, from the bottom of the hill.

"What are you going to do by yourself, Nalini?" Simon wanted to know. "Crawl home?"

"I can't carry you home, Grandma," Ruby said. The idea of Ruby even trying to carry Nalini was so comical that Zoe almost laughed.

"You most certainly can't!" protested Nalini. "I am *not* a sack of potatoes!"

So this is it, Zoe thought miserably, watching her brother walk away toward home. *This is how we get found out.*

As if she read Zoe's mind, Nalini called up the hill, "Sorry, Zoe." She was still sitting awkwardly in the snow, massaging her ankle.

"It's okay, don't worry. As long as you're all right."

"Of course I'm all right! It takes more than a twisted ankle to —"

"Oh no, Cinder! *Cinder!*"

Anna was staring helplessly at the blur of black fur racing down the hill, chasing a squirrel at top speed.

"Oh, no, no, no!" Anna cried. "How did I drop her leash *again?*"

Anna was suddenly running after Cinder in a panic, and William and Ruby followed. Even Ella ran off, chasing them.

That familiar helpless feeling crept into the pit of

Zoe's stomach. She could hear her friends' voices in the distance, calling Cinder. She could see Nalini alone in the snow. And there was nothing she could do.

Here I am, left out again. As soon as something happens, everyone leaves me alone! Why can't I run and help like everybody else?

Just then, Ella came back up the hill, looking puzzled and frustrated, and took her place at Zoe's side. But the dog kept looking from Zoe to Nalini and whining mournfully.

Zoe got over her bitterness, and came to her senses. She called down the hill, "Nalini, are you okay down there?"

"Zoe, send Ella down here with the push-broom. It's leaning on that tree beside you. I'm going to use it as a cane, so I can come to the top and wait with you."

Zoe couldn't believe her ears. "You're going to climb the hill with a twisted ankle? Stay put, Nalini, please."

"Stay put, my eye!"

So Zoe did as she was told. But it took a bit of doing.

Ella was determined not to leave Zoe again. She fetched the broom immediately when Zoe asked her, but she just stared when Zoe told her to take the broom to Nalini. Finally Zoe took the broom from Ella, lined it up and threw it down the hill as far as she could. It slid quite a long way, but skidded to a stop well out of Nalini's reach.

"Ella, go get the stick. Get the stick and take it to Nalini." Ella bounded after the "stick," grabbed one end of it and started back toward Zoe.

"No, no! Take the stick to Nalini," Zoe commanded, and Ella looked mystified. This was a strange game!

With both Zoe and Nalini talking to her, Ella got the point, and started dragging the broom down the hill. If Zoe hadn't been so busy coaching her wonderful dog, she would have laughed out loud. The broom was so big that Ella was practically walking sideways! Her eyes kept moving from Zoe to the broom, to Nalini, to Zoe....

✸✸✸

With a great deal of huffing and puffing, and dragging and groaning, Nalini made it up the hill leaning on her makeshift cane, with a worried dog beside her all the way.

As Nalini carefully lowered herself onto the snow at the top of the hill, she saw that Zoe was in tears.

"What's bothering you, Zoe?" she asked.

"My parents," Zoe wailed. "Now they'll know I've been tobogganing, and they'll never let me come here again. They'll say it's too dangerous. And they're going to be *so mad* about me sneaking out!"

Nalini smiled. "Well, I have to make a little confession," she said. "I called your mom and dad after the first time we came here, and I told them we were having some Sunday-morning fun together. I said it was our little secret."

Zoe was almost speechless. "You — you *told* them?"

"I had to. What if they'd woken up and found you gone? Think how much they would have worried! But I didn't give away our secret. I just promised to keep you safe and sound."

Nalini shifted uncomfortably, and rubbed her ankle. Zoe reflected on what she'd said. *Well, maybe I'm not in trouble for sneaking out. But that doesn't change the rest of it, she thought. They'll say, "See how dangerous it is?" They'll say, "If a grown-up like Nalini can get hurt, then you could get hurt." But I don't care if I get a little hurt! It's normal to get a little hurt sometimes! Why do I always have to be different?*

Once more, the tears welled up in her eyes. Her wonderful adventure was over. Her parents would never let her ride the toboggan again.

Chapter Eighteen
FLORA AND BEAU

"Nalini! Nalini! Nalini!"

What on earth…?

Lisa was running toward them, calling, gasping, out of breath. And she was wearing her *bathrobe*.

"Nalini…I don't know what…to do! Flora's loose in the living room. My parents went…to help…Grandma move out… and the babysitter's scared of birds. I *have* to get her back in the cage! But I don't know how! Beau can't fly, but Flora's zooming around and crashing into everything and I don't know what to do. Please come *quick!*"

127

Zoe put Ella in Lisa's bathroom with strict instructions to stay, and rubbed Ella's ears when the dog whimpered. Bathrooms reminded Ella of baths.

"It's okay, Ella. It's not bath time. I just need you out of the way so I can catch that bird without you two scaring each other. With Nalini hurt, and Simon away finding Dad, and everyone else chasing Cinder, there's no one left but me. I'll be back as soon as I can, I promise. Quiet down, please."

Reluctantly she turned and left the bathroom, closing the door firmly behind her and crossing her fingers. *I only have to do my best,* she told herself.

✗✗✗

As Zoe turned the corner from the bathroom, she saw a dipping, swerving blur that could only be Flora. After a minute, the bird landed on the back of the living room sofa, regarding Zoe and Lisa suspiciously, her head cocked to one side.

She seemed to be saying, *Well, well. Look who we have here. And by the way, aren't I gorgeous?*

Flora *was* a beautiful bird: mostly white, with bits of black on her wings, a patch of sunny yellow on her head and — best of all — a sky-blue chest.

Zoe looked at the chaos around her. Flora and Beau's cage was on a large stand in the kitchen, and inside it was Beau, a green and yellow parakeet, chirping nervously and flapping his flightless wings.

Sorry, Beau, Zoe thought to herself, but it's a good thing you can't fly. *The last thing we need is both of you loose in here.*

As for Flora, her feathers were everywhere. There were picture frames hanging lopsided on the wall. There was a ripped curtain on the window, where Flora must have landed. The floor was littered with bath towels, a shoe, a mop and two large hairbrushes. A real mess!

No wonder Lisa wants to get her back in the cage, Zoe thought. For the first time, she felt a little sympathy for her classmate.

"What *is* all this mess?" Zoe whispered.

Lisa rolled her eyes. "Natalie, the bonkers babysitter, was trying to corner Flora back into the cage with all those. She's bawling in the spare bedroom now, the scaredy cat."

Zoe looked again at the shoe, the hairbrushes, the towels, the mop. She tried to imagine Natalie lunging at the little bird with each of them. "What good would those do?" she murmured, to no one in particular. "Scaring her won't get her back in the cage. The poor bird must be freaking out!"

129

"Why are you whispering, anyway?"

"Because this will only work if we do it right. We have to stay calm and keep Flora calm. That's why."

Lisa looked doubtful. "I wish Grandma was here. Flora goes everywhere on her finger," she complained. "What can *you* do?"

Of course you don't think I can help, Zoe thought bitterly. *You don't think I can do anything!* Then she paused. What had Lisa just said about Flora going around on Grandma Carter's finger?

"Can you please clear this stuff off the floor, Lisa?" she asked, very quietly. "I can't get my wheelchair through to Flora with all this mess."

"What are you going to do?" Lisa whispered loudly, as she bent to pick up the shoe with one hand, and the mop with the other.

"I'm going to try to make friends."

✷✷✷

Slowly, carefully, speaking gently all the way, Zoe rolled her chair toward Flora. The bird kept darting away, but she seemed to like returning to perch on the back of the sofa. Zoe moved forward, bit by bit, in an awkward sort of dance, crooning and whistling softly as she went.

"That's it, that's a good girl. Flora's a good girl, a lovely bird, a good, lovely girl."

Zoe made her way toward Flora again and again, but whenever she got too close for Flora's comfort, the bird flew away and perched on the curtains, or on the windowsill, and Lisa let out a noisy, exasperated breath.

"This is ridiculous! What's the use?" Lisa asked.

"Patience, we need patience," Zoe answered, in a low, singsong voice.

Even though she too was frustrated, she could see that, gradually, Flora was beginning to trust her. Whenever the bird flew away from her, the distance was a little shorter than the time before. *I can do this!* Zoe caught herself thinking.

✼✼✼

Her patience was paying off. Flora was finally seriously thinking of landing on the finger that Zoe offered her as a perch. But just then, the babysitter, Natalie, burst out of the spare bedroom, brandishing an umbrella and shouting, *"GET BACK IN YOUR CAGE NOW, YOU DUMB BIRD, OR I'LL…I'LL…"*

In a flash, Flora took off and flew around in a frenzy. She landed on the very top of the curtain.

Zoe was too furious to whisper now. "Put that umbrella away! What's the matter with you? You've ruined *everything!*"

Natalie stormed back into the bedroom and slammed the door.

Ella, still in the bathroom, started whimpering again.

Zoe felt completely hopeless. *I shouldn't be here!* she thought.

Her stomach began to growl.

I haven't even had breakfast, she realized. *I'm hungry.*

Hungry?

Something clicked in her mind.

"Lisa, what does Flora like to eat?"

Lisa shrugged. "Birdseed, I think."

"But does she eat anything *besides* birdseed? Is there anything she likes *better?*"

A flash of understanding crossed Lisa's face. "She'll do anything for lettuce."

And that was how they managed it.

They started coaxing all over again, with Zoe holding a fresh green leaf of lettuce and Flora coming closer and closer and closer...closer...closer....

"I don't know why we didn't think of this earlier," Zoe said to Lisa, when Flora was perched on her finger and being inched toward the cage.

Lisa didn't speak for a moment, afraid to ruin their luck as Flora was finally eased into the cage.

YAHOO!

★★★

Zoe brought Ella out of the bathroom right away, now that it was safe. The dog looked so relieved that Zoe wanted to cry.

"Can I pet her?" Lisa asked shyly.

After a small pause, Zoe said, "Sure."

Not long after, Lisa said something so quietly that at first Zoe was sure she had imagined it. "*You* thought of it, Zoe. You did it. I didn't think you could. I thought we were doomed when I found out Nalini couldn't help. She fixes everything!"

"Oh, I know!" Zoe agreed.

There was an awkward silence. Then:

"Zoe, can I tell you something?"

"Yeah."

"I've been seeing you tobogganing from my bedroom window."

Zoe felt herself get all prickly. "And?"

"Oh, nothing. I...I...was just wondering why I never saw you out of your wheelchair before. I didn't know you could…get out of it. The wheelchair, I mean. At school you never do."

"I get out of my chair all the time at home. I'm afraid of kids at school staring, I guess. I hate it when people stare. But I think I know now that some people will always stare, and I just have to get on with having fun. Let them look if they want to! It doesn't matter that I do some things differently than other people."

Silence fell again. And then Lisa asked:

"Do you think I should tell Natalie she can come out now?"

She answered her own question, just as Zoe did.

"Nah!" they chorused, and both collapsed into giggles.

Chapter Nineteen

FREE AS A BIRD

"Would you like to hold Beau until your mom gets here?" Lisa's grandmother wanted to know. She had given Zoe a huge bowl of cereal, and thanked her about ten times for helping Lisa with Flora. "Beau can't fly away, dear, and he's a very sweet bird."

Zoe had never felt anything as soft as Beau's feathers. She stroked and stroked him, and when he fell asleep in her palm, she felt honored to the tips of her toes.

What was it Nalini had said the day she put henna on Zoe's hands? *You don't know everything these hands will do.* As usual, Nalini had been right.

"Ah, he must have you thinking he's the quiet one, taking a nap like this!" Grandma Carter said, as she sat beside Zoe.

"What do you mean?"

"I mean, don't let Beau fool you. He can be full of spunk too, even though he doesn't fly. I take him out of his cage a lot, and let him peck all the tiles, and chirp at Flora and the birds outside. I take him with me all the time, on my finger, on my shoulder…sometimes even on my head! He loves my curls. They're his own little jungle!"

Zoe giggled, picturing Grandma Carter with a bird on her head, pecking through her curls. Then she thought of something else.

"You let Flora out too, right? Or it wouldn't be fair."

"Yes, I let her out a lot. That's why her wings are so strong. But she's not the only one having a good time. Flora has fun because she can fly high and go where she wants to. Beau has fun because he gets to see the world I see, and he doesn't always have to go back in his cage. Flora travels on my finger, but only indoors. Anytime I take her away from home, she needs to be in the cage, and see everything through the bars. With Beau, it's different."

"Because he can't just fly away?"

"That's right. Sometimes we go shopping in the market together. All my friends know him, and he sits on their shoulders too. He loves the adventure, all the sights and sounds of the world. My finger is his subway train and his elevator. We watch television together, and

I even read to him. He thinks stories are wonderful! And in the summer I give him baths. He loves water."

"So do I," Zoe said.

Grandma Carter smiled and leaned toward Zoe, whispering, "Don't tell Lisa this. She'll worry too much. But since I know he won't escape, sometimes I put Beau in the grass to play. I sit close by and watch out for cats, and he gets to do what he likes best: soak up the sun, and chase bugs and worms and caterpillars."

"He must have a great time!"

"He does. Oh sure, Flora can fly free, and see from way up high. But Beau's a lucky bird too. He's my buddy."

Beau is just like me, Zoe thought. *He can't fly, and it's easy to think his life is boring. But he gets adventures all the time! His are just different from Flora's, that's all. And he's making me so happy! If he could fly…if he could fly, he wouldn't be in my hand right now.*

✦✦✦

As her mother drove her home, telling her that Cinder was safe and Nalini would be just fine, Zoe kept waiting for the scolding about how upset her parents were because of her secret tobogganing. She kept waiting for the news that she must never, ever do that again.

Her first surprise was that the warning didn't come.

Her second surprise came when her mother stopped the car at the entrance to the park.

Her father and Simon were waiting there — and they had Nalini's toboggan!

"Well," Zoe's mother explained, as Zoe stared, "what with one thing and another, you didn't get your toboggan ride this morning. Want to go now?"

Ella woofed and wagged her tail.

Zoe smiled from ear to ear. She smiled big and wide and true, so very thankful for life and all its good parts.

ACKNOWLEDGMENTS

I most gratefully acknowledge the financial assistance of the Ontario Arts Council and the indispensable support and guidance of the following individuals: Margie Wolfe, Gena K. Gorrell, Carolyn Jackson, Ken Setterington, Brenda Halliday, Barbara Greenwood, Gillian O'Reilly, Michelle Benincasa, Susan Guenther, Dr. Joanne Harris Burgess, Dr. Cyril Greenland, Grace Feuerverger, Tina Bauer, John and Ann Bauer, Elizabeth and James Watt, Nalini Singh, Mindy Thuna, Kathy Kacer, Nicole and Keith Farrar, and Frances and Mike Minaki.

It takes a village to plant the seeds of a book. The unwavering encouragement and inspiring examples of the rest of my village have helped me put Zoe to paper with confidence: Rie Yamagishi, Vanessa Belonio, Nisha Batra, Heather and Mike Cameron, Kevin Williams, Monique Hodge, Jillian Dempsey, Shirley Lauder, Ruthann Hionides-Garcia, Tara Geraghty, Georgia Caruso, Bonnie Mathisen, Anthony Styga, Pam Quirk, Terry Milligan, Alison McCullough, and Sukanti Iyne-Husain.

REFERENCES

Barkin, Carol, & Elizabeth James. *The Holiday Handbook*. New York: Clarion Books, 1994.

Burnstein, Chaya M. *The Jewish Kids Catalogue*. Philadelphia: The Jewish Publication Society, 1993.

Feuerverger, G. *Oasis of Dreams: Teaching and Learning Peace in a Jewish-Palestinian Village in Israel*. New York: RoutledgeFalmer, 2001.

Goss, Linda, & Clay Goss. *It's Kwanzaa Time*. New York: G.P. Putnam's Sons, 1994.

Jones, Lynda. *Kids around the World Celebrate: The Best Feasts and Festivals from Many Lands*. New York: John Wiley & Sons, Inc., 2000.

Kadodwala, Dilip. *A World of Holidays: Divali*. Austin: Steck-Vaughn Company, 1998.

Pandya, Meenal. *Here Comes Divali, the Festival of Lights*. Wellesley, MA: MeeRa Publications, 2001.

Peterson, Eugene H. *The Message: The Bible in Contemporary Language*. Colorado: Navpress Publishing Group, 2002.

Rosen, Mike. *Winter Festivals*. East Sussex, U.K.: Wayland Publisher's Limited, 1990.

Sadlier, Rosemary. *The Kids Book of Black Canadian History*. Toronto: Kids Can Press, 2003.

Susan Kantor, ed. *An Illustrated Treasury of African American Read-Aloud Stories*. New York: Black Dog & Leventhal Publishers, 2003.

Thomas, P. *Festivals and Holidays of India*. Bombay: D.B. Taraporevela & Co., 1971.

Waggoner, Susan. *It's a Wonderful Christmas: The Best of the Holidays, 1940-1965*. New York: Stewart, Tabori & Chang, 2004.

Washington, Donna L. *The Story of Kwanzaa*. New York: HarperCollins Publishers, 1996.

www.hennapage.com

www. hennacaravan.com

www. visittnt.com/ToDo/Events/Divali/origin.htm

www3.kumc.edu/diversity/ethnic_relig/diwali.html

www.sscnet.ucla.edu/southasia/Culture/Festivals/Diwali.html

www.jewfaq.org/holiday7.htm

www.holidays.net/ramadan/story.htm

www.submission.org/YES/YES-2.html

www.submission.org/YES/child2.html